The First Witness of "Nazi Gold"

The First Witness of "Nazi Gold"

by

Steven Wassermann

Copyright © 2000 by Steven Wassermann

All rights reserved. No part of this book may be reproduced, stored in a retrieval system, or transmitted by any means, electronic, mechanical, photocopying, recording, or otherwise, without written permission from the author.
Published by
1st Books Library LLC, 2000
Park Horizon Publishing LLC, 1999

ISBN 1-58500-797-8

1stbooks – rev. 5/19/00

ABOUT THE BOOK

YOU WANT TO READ SOMETHING DIFFERENT!

The saga of Jewish resistance from within the **HOLOCAUST**.

This is an **ACTION STORY** not a "tear-jerker".

A historical and eye-witness account of courageous **JEWISH OPPOSITION TO NAZI GERMANY**.

SABOTAGE PLAN. Young men, hardly more than boys, forge and execute a plan to stop supplies from reaching the German troops on the Eastern front.

The ingenious plan of the first discovery of the existence and trail of the **"NAZI GOLD"**.

Description of how the Nazis plotted to hide the conditions in Dachau from the **INTERNATIONAL RED CROSS** inspectors.

SPYING FROM WITHIN THE CONCENTRATION CAMP.

The first-hand description of the little known activity to gather and pass-on valuable strategic information to the Allies from within Dachau.

This book will make every fair minded person applaud the success of the "underdog".

PROLOGUE	ix
"ACHTUNG" EXPLOSIVES!!	1
A GOOD NIGHT'S REST	7
A LOAF OF BREAD	11
HUNGARIAN BREAD	15
MEETING THE GERMANS	17
DAVID AND GOLIATH	21
A VOYAGE TO THE UNKNOWN	37
THE TRIP TO DACHAU	45
THE "GHOST TRAIN"	49
A VISIT TO THE KREMATORIUM	55
TRICKY CHOICE	59
A FEW CIGARETTES FOR A LIFE	63
MEETING AN OLD FRIEND	71
THE GAMBLE	73
INFORMATION GATHERING (SPYING)	75
THE PHONE CALL	85
THE "NAZI GOLD"	89
DECEIVING THE RED CROSS	105
MINOR SURGERY	111
CRIME AND PUNISHMENT?	117
ESCAPE!!! SAVING A GOOD LIFE	119
THE LIBERATION	137
DANGER HIGH VOLTAGE!	143
WAR CRIMES TRIALS	147
"DOES HE HAVE A GUN?"	153
MORE VISITORS	171
POSTSCRIPT	175
APPENDIX	177

PROLOGUE

It was 1934. I was about ten years old. I had just finished the compulsory four-year elementary school and had a little more time to be with my parents. I noticed the hours usually set aside by my parents after supper for listening to the radio were spent, instead, on long discussions about my future. The immediate subject was the selection of a proper "gymnasium" to prepare me for university studies. "GYMNASIUM"" in Hungary and in many countries of Europe was the name and definition of a secondary school (high school) of eight years duration, preparing students to enter a university.

They decided (hoped) I would become a physician (two sons of older brothers of my father were physicians). Toward that end they felt the most appropriate school was the "classical gymnasium" in the 7th District of Budapest. Since we lived in the 6th District, my father had to use all his connections to get me admitted to that school. This school offered eight years of Latin and four years of Greek as an elective, a highly concentrated classical education which supposedly prepared better for medicine than curriculums of other types of high schools.

I entered the school and was always among the best students in my class.

Although the official religion of Hungary was Roman Catholic, public high schools in those days offered religious education to students of the three major religions. Catholic, Protestant (mostly Calvinist and some Lutheran) and Jewish. In my school close to half of the students were Jewish.

ix

Like most Jews in Hungary I believed that my nationality was Hungarian and my religion Jewish.

Eight years is a long time and the world changed. During 1938 Hitler attacked Poland. Due to the proximity, influence and aggressive behavior of Nazi Germany the Hungarian government (with some notable exceptions) became more and more anti-Semitic and the proposition of duality of nationality and religion was no longer accepted. A Jew was a Jew and not a Hungarian.

My parents' original plans for my future appeared to be going up in smoke.

I also disappointed my parents somewhat, because during the early years in the gymnasium I realized my talents lay in the fields of mathematics and physics and decided on a future in the engineering sciences.

I was in my last year of high school in 1942. The chances of any Jew being admitted to a university to study medicine, engineering or anything else became zero. The Hungarian laws governing the admission of Jews to the universities started with the so called *"numerus clausus"*, or limited (closed) numbers, and by 1942 they were followed by the *"numerus nullus"*, or zero, no Jews admitted at all. In spite of all this, I (and most other Jewish high school graduates) neatly filled out all the necessary forms for university admission including the attachment of my high school certificate of graduation with honors.

I almost forgot to mention the first question on the admission form, after the name, was religion. I could not explain the reason for going through with the unnecessary formality of applying, knowing that my chances of admission were zero. It must have been the consequence of an inner drive to prove to myself that in my studies I accomplished all I set out to do and went as far as circumstances permitted. Some weeks later, on the first specified date, I took the subway and the streetcar to the university. My first glance went to the **W**-s and, as expected, my name was not included. I was not surprised. Sad, but not surprised. As I started to study the names of those admitted I ran across the name of a Gentile classmate. That fellow failed the final exam of the gymnasium. The subject he failed was mathematics (and this was a college of engineering)! He was admitted to the engineering school before having taken the make-up exam in high school. It was more important to be a Gentile than to be talented, but that was surely no news. As I was standing in front of the announcement board with tears in the corners of my eyes, I was silently wondering what it meant to be the "Chosen People". The news of the college rejection was no surprise at home.

The laws, called "JEW LAWS", and the mood of the Hungarian population against the Jews became more and more oppressive and ugly.

On one cool, rainy and windy fall afternoon, my father came home earlier than usual and was visibly agitated and shaken.

"I spent about an hour with your uncle Joseph", he said and paused. My uncle's claim to fame was that as a sergeant in World War I, he was awarded the highest military medal of the Austro-Hungarian Monarchy (equivalent to the Congressional Medal of Honor) for bravery in action beyond the call of duty. Because of that, he was (temporarily) exempt from all (or most) JEW-LAWS. (He later perished in Auschwitz.) "Your uncle has connections at high places and he was told the government considers several areas of preferential treatment for those Jews who convert to Catholicism". Do you want to convert?"

Several of my friends had converted and conversions became frequent among Jews in Budapest. In spite of this, my father's question was unexpected and I knew it broke his heart to bring it over his lips. "I was born a Jew and plan to die as one," I answered. Nothing further was said. My father blew his nose and gazed through the rain splattered window. The subject was closed and never mentioned again.

The only concern of the Hungarian Jews was to improve their chances of survival. We still hoped (foolishly) that the Nazis would not occupy Hungary, but, at least in hindsight, this was a naive and irrational dream considering the tremendous power of the Germans and the strong pro-Nazi sentiment within certain circles in Hungary.

It was widely known that Admiral Miklos Horthy, the Head of State (Regent) of Hungary, hated the Nazis almost as much as he hated communists, but no rationally thinking person could imagine that he could successfully confront them.

What do we do to improve our chances of survival? Segregating ourselves from the Hungarian majority appeared to be a plan that could only end in disaster. The overall consensus of the Jews which ultimately prevailed could be summed up in four words: "make ourselves economically useful". Jews in Hungary were intellectuals, lawyers, physicians, scientists, and, of course, first and foremost, merchants. As a matter of fact, a vast segment of the Hungarian middle class was Jewish. This was the position which made us envied (and thus disliked) by the masses. The thought occurred to the Jews that useful occupations in the trades would make us more acceptable to the Hungarians. This also fitted with the argument that, should a German occupation of Hungary come to pass, professions valuable to the German war effort may keep us alive.

"I think you should start an apprenticeship in a technical trade" my father said one day. Luckily a friend of a friend had a large precision machine shop in the outskirts of Budapest. Owning and operating a machine shop was not common among Jews, although Hungary's two largest, and most prestigious machinery factories were owned and managed by Jews. We grabbed the opportunity when Mr. Szanter agreed to take me on as an apprentice. Incidentally the number of Jewish apprentices that he could hire was also fixed by law. There were about ten apprentices in the shop. I was the only Jew. Apprenticeship was a cast system. Work and other assignments depended not only on the seniority of the apprentice, but also on undefined and arbitrary procedures.

The work-week for masters and journeymen was five and a half days, the half-day was Saturday. The apprentices, however, worked six days. We cleaned the shop Saturday afternoon after all of the others had left. The job consisted of cleaning and oiling all machinery and tools, sweeping the floors, disposing, in barrels, hundreds of pounds of metal chips accumulated during the week and cleaning toilets.

Andras, the senior apprentice, was in charge of cleaning. For two reasons he did his best to make my life miserable. I am not sure what his "dislike" priorities were. He surely did not like the idea I was a high school graduate, because that reduced my apprenticeship years to less than two years, from the three years applicable to him. Further, judging from the Hungarian Nazi papers he was reading and continuously quoting from, he was a violent anti-Semite.

On the first Saturday afternoon, after most of the clean-up was done, Andras turned to me and barked "Steve, clean the toilets and use all the elbow-grease you have. I will come in and check in an hour".

I took the pails, brushes, brooms, cleaning materials and entered the rest room. It stank terribly! I opened the doors of the booths and realized none of the toilets had been flushed and all windows were closed. It did not take much imagination to realize Andras put some of the apprentices up to play this trick on me. I did not complain or say anything. I cleaned and did the best job I could do. While doing it, I was grinding my teeth in anger and bitterness thinking how circumstances had changed since we discussed my future in medicine with my parents, some years ago.

What all Hungarian Jews were afraid of came to pass when Hungary was occupied by the Germans on March 17, 1944.

At just about the same time my apprenticeship was completed, and I had to undergo the usual test to become a journeyman mechanic. My test, however, was anything but usual. In the general course of events, and to render the evaluation objective, the test usually took place in a shop other than where the apprenticeship was served. The site of test was chosen by the Trade Federation of Mechanics and was, in most instances, a machine shop engaged in work similar to where the apprenticeship was served.

When I learned the place of my test, I continued to realize all happenings were viciously directed against us Jews. The site of the test was one of the most openly anti-Semitic and German managed companies in Hungary: BOSCH, A.G.

They did everything in their power to make me fail the test, but their approach went wrong. The subject of my test was machining work requiring complex computations. They were sure very few graduating apprentices could handle such tasks. They miscalculated with me. They could have failed me easily with jobs requiring manual dexterity, but mathematics was my forte. I passed the exam, to their dismay, with flying colors. They gave me a C, or the lowest passing mark.

The Germans made their presence felt immediately and the Hungarian government had no choice but to cooperate. Some Hungarian Nazi factions cooperated not only willingly, but enthusiastically.

Jewish males were conscripted into forced labor brigades, many of which ended up in Auschwitz.

By the end of the war, about 570,000 Hungarian Jews perished including most of my relatives. I have extremely fond memories of my uncles Miklos and Joseph, my aunt Olga and her daughter, my cousin Kati, whom I loved like a sister. None of them came back after the war. My aunt Olga and my cousin Kati were seen by some of their neighbors, who survived. These witnesses related that my aunt was with them in Auschwitz when they all recognized her daughter Kati dead on top of a heap of corpses. The sight instantly drove my aunt out of her mind. She was subsequently gassed. Kati was seventeen years old when the Nazis killed her. She was an excellent scholar who spoke five languages fluently. She had the slender figure of a trained ballet dancer and was the sweetest person you could ever know.

My uncle Miklos was known to have been alive shortly before the end of the war, but perished in one of the infamous "prisoner marches" directed by the Nazis.

Fortunately my parents survived the Holocaust, having been hidden by Gentile friends and by hiding in attics and coal-bins in cellars.

During May of 1944 I received my notice of conscription into forced labor. I was to report to a Hungarian military base at the village of Jolsva, not far from the town of Miskolc. I remember no details of how I left our apartment, or how I got to Jolsva. Neither faces nor events of those days are preserved in my memory.

The first window in my memory was our arrival at Jolsva. Tens of thousand of Jews were continuously arriving by trains. We were ordered off the trains and were milling around in an area the size of several soccer fields. For hours after my arrival, there was no activity at all. Additional trains were arriving and the only distraction was to try to find familiar faces in the crowd. Finally I recognized a friend from Budapest, the son of a well known pediatrician with offices on "Oktogon" (Octagon) Square, close to where we lived. George and I attended elementary school together and, although we ended up in different high schools, we kept up the childhood friendship and visited each other often. Meeting him was one of the best things that happened to me because George was an incorrigible optimist, great company during such oppressive days.

After a while, loudspeakers instructed us to divide into two groups, Jews and Converted-Jews. George and I looked at each other questioningly. Then, without uttering a word, we started to move toward the area specified for Jews. George smiled and said: "let us see how well 'chosen' we are".

Our yellow Stars of David, which all Jews had to wear in Hungary, were changed for yellow arm-bands for Jews and white arm-bands for converted Jews.

I never inquired, or followed up, whether the converted Jews had a better fate during the Holocaust than those of us who were willing to risk our lives for the principle.

"ACHTUNG" EXPLOSIVES!!

A few weeks after I was called in to forced labor service, theoretically a part of the Hungarian Army, the disorganized mass of thousands of Jews were formed into "regiments" consisting of four companies each. The regiments were quartered in a variety of buildings consisting of railroad storage buildings, railroad waiting rooms, farmers' sheds and stalls, etc. My company shared accommodations and straw to sleep on with several sheep and goats in a farmer's stall.

The regiments, at that time just in the process of being organized, were not given permanent assignments or specific locations. Thousands of Jewish laborers worked on random assignments (often "make-work") at, or around the railroad station of Miskolc.

The main claim to fame of this town was (except its picturesque location at the foot-hills of the Carpathian Mountains) that it was an important rail junction about 100 miles north-east of Budapest on the main railroad line to the Eastern Front. As will become clear later, most of the time during this period of my life revolved around the railroad.

The night bombings of the Allies succeeded in destroying or damaging tracks, rail-beds, rolling stock and first and foremost locomotives. As a consequence, many trains were trapped because they ended up on stretches of the tracks which were destroyed at both ends of the trains.

Our task at that time was to locate damaged or "stuck" railroad freight cars and inventory their contents.

The second phase was to transfer the contents of the damaged or trapped cars (cars standing on dead-ended rail sections) to freight cars which were pushed on the still useable tracks as close to the trapped cars as possible.

This freight car shunting operation was done almost exclusively by human-power for two reasons. The first was that there were only a very few locomotives. The second reason was that in order to move freight cars from one track to another we had to put down improvised spurs and switches which could hardly take the weight of empty cars and surely could not have taken the weights of locomotives.

Originally, at times of Allied air raids, our guards allowed us to disperse, which for all practical purposes meant to run as far as possible from the rail yard and hide under trees, in sheds, or just lie on the ground in gullies. As the number of air raids increased, the Hungarian military decided that work must go on during air raids. Fortunately for the Allied war effort, but unfortunately for us, the accuracy of the Allied bombings became better by the day. A contributing factor was that the German-Hungarian air defenses became weaker as time went on. The only thing we could do was to seek shelter in freight cars. This was no help in the event of a direct hit, but saved many of us from serious injury from flying objects.

The injured or dead were taken to a designated building marked on the roof by a large red cross. Not coincidentally, the building also housed the local German and Hungarian military commands as well as the command post of the railroad administration.

Once the freight cars were located and placed according to plan, we were ordered to transfer the contents of the trapped cars to the cars standing on useable tracks.

Moving, locating and arranging the freight cars required planning and skill and it was directed in a reasonable and entirely humane manner by Hungarian railroad officials and workers.

In contrast, the supervision of the unloading and reloading required no brain power, only an adequate amount of innate brutality, and was performed by Hungarian soldiers and mainly by gendarmes (recognizable from the feather on their caps). We Jews tried to help each other by moving the older and weaker people to cars containing relatively easy-to-handle loads. The young ones took on the sometimes unbelievably heavy bulk items. The simplest to describe, and one that I will always remember, was bags full of beans weighing 80 kg (176 pounds) each. Luckily I did not have to lift them; (I could not have). I was just standing with my back toward the door of a freight car and others pushed the bag to me. I reached over my shoulders, grabbed two corners of the bag and walked it (very gently) to the door of a freight car standing on useable tracks. Here I backed to the open door and let the bag slide to the floor of the car.

All of the above resulted in deaths and injuries which we started to get accustomed to.

Frequently, next night's bombings rendered the entire work useless by destroying more tracks.

One morning a special "selection" took place. About 80-100 of us moved out, all young men. After arriving at the railroad station we were marched to an area crisscrossed by many rail tracks. This was the marshaling section of the station. We observed armed Hungarian soldiers in the distance forming what appeared to be a large perimeter all around us. We were made to stop at a secluded spot behind a large locomotive switching building. A young Hungarian army corporal arranged us in a large circle and told us that some of the Allied aerial bombs did not explode upon impact. However, these were still dangerous and might go off from vibration or the least shock and represented a danger for the German rail traffic. (In those days most rolling stock on this line carried either German soldiers or equipment to or from the Russian front.) Our job would be to defuse these bombs and subsequently to remove them. From a canvas bag he took some mechanical parts and identified them as parts of the explosive-head of the bombs. He pointed to a screw and explained that this must be removed to defuse the bomb, after which it could be safely transported. He stressed that the danger increased the closer you got to the explosion trigger, because the least movement could activate it.

One of the Jews asked whether this meant that the bomb must be completely dug out, since it was likely that it had fallen nose first and bored itself into the ground. The corporal said that the bombs appeared to be tumbling in the air and that he personally had defused several bombs which were buried horizontally or even tip up in the ground. He added that our job will be limited to exposing the bomb very carefully and retreating from the site and calling him. He would do the defusing.

There were eight or ten locations, most of them appearing as small craters, but some looked like small hills, where unexploded bombs were suspected.

We were divided into equal groups and given shovels. Then each group marched off to an area of an unexploded bomb site marked by sticks of wood in the ground.

In my area nothing was visible except a crater with some splintered wood railroad ties in it. In order to avoid having to go down and move around at the bottom of the hole, we improvised long sticks and drove several large nails into one end of the stick with the pointy ends of the nails sticking out. By swinging these tools with nails down we succeeded in hooking most of the splintered rail ties and pulled them up from the crater.

Then the time for digging came. We decided that at any time only two of us would go down into the hole to dig. The rest would lie on the ground a safe distance away. According to our corporal, 15-20 meters (about 50 feet), possibly behind small ground elevations, was safe.

I was in the second or third pair of diggers. After some very ginger exploring and lifting out some shovels full of dirt, my partner thought that his shovel had touched on something hard. We instantly threw the shovels up and out of the hole and continued to scrape the ground with scraps of wood and with our fingers. It appeared safer to distribute our weight by lying down. This also prevented us from accidentally stepping on something sensitive or tipping or jarring the mostly buried bomb with our weight. We wiggled around and removed the dirt from around the bomb by the hand-full. It was an eerie feeling and I guess we continued only because we were hardened by the despair of our situation. We continued because we thought that our end would come sooner or later, anyhow. After a few minutes it became obvious that we were touching metal. Both of us were shaky and sweated profusely and decided to give up and report our findings to the corporal.

This, however, never came to pass.

As we were crawling out of the hole an explosion shook the area. We found out that another team had discovered an unexploded bomb a few minutes earlier and had called the corporal. Before he instructed all the Jews to take cover, he selected one of them to help him in defusing the bomb.

Both of them died instantly.

The young corporal was one of the most decent Hungarian military men I have met. He did not discriminate. He did not chase Jews to their deaths and he was ready to sacrifice his own life for what he understood to be in the service of his country.

I hope both of them rest in peace.

Tragically, this was only the beginning of our misfortunes. Before we were transferred from the Miskolc area 10-15 of our comrades died while assisting in defusing "unexploded" bombs. The most dreadful single incident was when a small group of my friends (I shared breakfast a few minutes before with one of them) handled a bomb which was thought to have been properly defused. Suddenly, the bomb exploded with a horrendous roar. We could feel the vibration of the blast hundreds of feet away.

Parts of human bodies, clothing, shower of blood, clumps of earth, fragments of steel covered an area of about 100 feet in every direction.

While we collected the remains there were no Jewish eyes left dry. Our hands and entire bodies were shaking as we put the, mostly unrecognizable, parts of bodies into a single wooden crate. As one of our comrades led us in prayers, (while the Hungarian guards withdrew a few hundred feet). we lowered the remains into a freshly dug grave, near the top of a small hill, overlooking the railroad station.

We have cut a square wood board, drew a Star of David on it and wrote the names within.

Another sad and lonely memorial to the Holocaust.

A GOOD NIGHT'S REST

We were abruptly commanded to a different section of the railroad recently damaged by Allied bombs which also trapped a freight train of military importance for the Germans. The stretch of the railroad track was far from any inhabited area. There was not even a small village near-by. Our work-unit was in the process of taking up quarters in a group of abandoned and dilapidated farmers' sheds. There were no utilities or sanitary facilities. We were ordered to dig a long trench which served as a latrine.

For the first few days, a small pond covered with green algae was our only source of water for washing and drinking. We were told that a truck would bring in large containers of water and replenish the water supply daily. Of course, we had no idea whether this was really planned, but as it turned out it really did happen.

Drinking water was available at the work zone at the tracks, brought in by a hand-operated truck which moved on the rails. We even had our own water boy (most originally and affectionately referred to as Gunga Din) who walked along the work area with a pail of water and metal drinking cups. Smuggling water back to the camp was severely punished. This was completely senseless, arbitrary and capricious and the only way to explain it was that the commander assumed that he could control people more easily if their water was rationed.

It must have been the second day at that location when we decided to boil some water from the pond for drinking and washing. There were plenty of large containers in the kitchen and we collected dry wood and started to make a fire.

Hardly had we started the fire when the commanding officer, a Hungarian army captain, rushed out of his tent cracking his horse whip. We had never seen him without it. He was hollering from the top of his lungs, calling us traitors because the fire was obviously a signal to the Allied airmen. We were confounded (to say the least) because kitchen fires were burning all day anyhow and because it was still daylight, well before sun-down, and our camp was at least three miles from the closest point of the railroad.

Some of the fellows ran for cover back into the sheds, but since the noise had brought out several Hungarian guards, about ten of us got stuck in the clearing to face the ranting and raving commander. Suddenly he simmered down and told us to go and collect saplings in a near-by grove. He specified about fifty pieces of wood not less than six feet long.

We thought we had got away real easy It took us a couple of hours to get back to camp with the wood and one of the Hungarian soldiers who supervised us went to call the commander.

He came with a furtive smile on his face and ordered us to stand in a small circle around him, as if to make sure that we heard and understood him. He announced in the most formal manner that we would not get supper and at "lights out" (we had a small generator feeding about a dozen light bulbs) we were to put the sticks which we had collected across the latrine trench and sleep on them.

He assigned some Hungarian guards who ended up watching us all night from a safe distance.

It was a warm summer night and the stench was overwhelming. It was a distinct advantage that we had had no supper. Obviously none of us slept, being afraid of falling into the ----trench.

It was during this night and in whispered conversations that the idea of our revenge was born and started to take shape.

A LOAF OF BREAD

It was summer of 1944.

Our Jewish (forced) labor regiment in Hungary was, as usual, working on repairing railroads destroyed by Allied bombers. We were in the area of Komarom (Komorno), a small town situated between Vienna and Budapest. The line was one of the main rail support arteries of the southern part of the Eastern front which, at that time, was the scene of major Russian offensives and advances.

Our "regiment" consisted of about 300-400 Jews working, and about 40 Hungarian officers, non-commissioned officers and soldiers supervising. In effect, the Jews were worker/prisoners and the Hungarian military were jailers.

The first phase of our task was to repair the rail bed, consisting of grading the ground and covering it with crushed stone. The second stage of the work was to set railroad ties and new rails into place. After that we drove in the spikes and installed the connecting strips and the bolts. Because of the warm weather we had to consider the expansion of the rails in the summer heat and the work had to be done near sunrise, before the rails expanded from the heat.

We moved out from our make-shift barracks at between 3-4 in the morning and put the rail sections into their proper positions with the connecting strips loosely tightened by about 10 a.m. Clearly, our work-day was not over at that time and we continued with a phase of work called, in the Hungarian railroad vernacular, "krampacsolas" (a word hard even for a Hungarian to pronounce). The closest English equivalent is tamping, which denotes the compacting of the crushed rock under the wood ties. The work was performed with a heavy blunt-ended modified hoe and its purpose was to drive the crushed rock firmly under the wooden railroad ties to create a strong bed of support. The work was an unbelievable strain on the back and performing it for six to eight hours daily after lugging rails for the previous six to eight hours made cripples of many of us. One company of our regiment, of which I was a member, consisted of 19-20 year old youngsters, the other three were middle-aged Jews, most of whom had never done any hard physical work in their lives. This resulted in 25% of our brigade having to do almost 100% of the work to avoid the penalties associated with not completing the daily work quota.

The Hungarian officers, who, incidentally, were absolutely no experts in building railroads, established stiff daily quotas in terms of hundreds of yards of rails to be completed. The quotas depended on real or imaginary needs and were often determined by whether the war-news on the radio was good or bad for the Germans and the Hungarians. In the event of bad news, a few extra hundred yards were added as "punishment".

One day a small contingent of us was ordered to repair a rural dirt road to allow trucks to bring building materials closer to our railroad work area. To get to the damaged part of the road we had to cross a small overpass above the Vienna-Budapest highway. On the highway below us was an endless stream of people moving slowly in a westerly direction. Since our guards, one officer and two soldiers, were left behind us, we stopped to take a close look at the people marching on the highway. The yellow stars clearly indicated that this was a group of Jews being herded toward the Austrian border. As I kept looking down, a familiar face lifted toward me and I recognized my uncle Sandor Rosner. "We had a bowl of soup a day since we started from Budapest; we are starving", he cried out. I reached into my bag, pulled out my left-over bread ration and threw it down to him.

I noticed movement from the corner of my eye. The lieutenant caught up with us and was standing there with legs spread and revolver in hand aimed at me. He had apparently witnessed the whole incident.

"Dirty Jew, are you not afraid that I will shoot you?" hollered the lieutenant. I snapped to attention and uttered only a single word-- "NO". Luckily, he probably realized that a live young working Jew would do more for the railroad than a dead one lying on the overpass. He changed his mind and was satisfied with a lesser punishment such as some lashes on my bare legs with his riding stick.

Ever since, I have often asked myself how honest my response to the lieutenant was. Was I really not afraid when I looked into the muzzle of the gun? There is no doubt that if I had gotten into a similar situation after the war, even while at a young age, or ever since, I would have been frightened out of my wits. If I could have come up with any answer at all, it surely would not have been "no". However, at that time, when death was all around me and my life was hanging on a thin thread at all times, my answer was spontaneous and natural. I really meant it.

The westward march of my uncle was likely his last. Nobody heard from him since. A victim of the Holocaust. Maybe I gave him his last piece of bread.

HUNGARIAN BREAD

It was an especially tough day. We were both laying tracks and filling embankments. While laying rails could be done only very early in the morning before the steel expanded from the heat of the day, the restoring of embankments and rail beds destroyed by bombs could be done at all hours. Doing both tasks amounted to a very long day, from about 4 a.m. to near sunset.

As we were moving back to camp, some of us decided to leave the narrow winding dirt path and walked straight through the wheat fields. It was past reaping time and the wheat was already collected and piled into neat pyramids. Naturally, some odd sticks of what remained uncollected were lying on the ground. I was much too tired and most certainly did not notice where I stepped.

I don't know which came first, the whip-lash or the voice. "You dirty Jew, you are stepping on sacred Hungarian bread". (This is a verbatim translation, neither the sound nor the voice will I ever forget). He was the top sergeant who, although not an officer, commanded one of our companies because he was the assigned representative of the Hungarian Nazi party, the "Arrow-Crosses".

About half a dozen whip lashes followed to the back of my legs. My knees buckled under me. Two comrades came to my aid. Half leaning on them, half being dragged, I got back to the camp.

Luckily the sergeant disappeared, probably to indulge in his usually overwhelming quota of peach brandy.

At the request of one of the fellows who helped me, a Hungarian corporal who was either supervising the kitchen or had a day off came to see me. He turned back, walked to his tent and returned with an army shirt soaked in cold water which he put on my legs. It felt good and I thanked him.

Later that day the first-aid man of our regiment looked at me and decided to give me one day of kitchen duty as a recovery period.

This incident is just an example, the sergeant's brutality and brutality in general were typical daily occurrences. I am lucky that I got away as easily as I did.

MEETING THE GERMANS

During the early fall of 1944 we were moved south-east toward the Danube. The Russian offensive had succeeded in moving into Hungary and the Germans and Hungarians were planning to use the river as a line of defense. At our new position our Jewish labor brigade was within the war zone and exposed to Russian artillery fire, Allied air attacks and, first and foremost, German and Hungarian brutality. Our quarters were abandoned farm houses of the local villagers who had fled to escape being caught in the cross-fire of the battle front.

Until we arrived at this station, our work schedule always appeared to have been planned and organized. This time everything was a picture of complete confusion. Assignments changed two or three times a day, with the result that nothing got completed. Material was piled up for roads which never got built, concrete was poured for overpasses for which there was no steel to complete them, military vehicles were pulled out of marsh-land along the Danube at great effort, only for it to be realized that they were damaged beyond repair. Trains were moving on a single track line in opposite directions, resulting in delays and at times the complete local breakdown of the German military rail movement.

We were ordered to repair major damage on a small railroad bridge. The materials were to be salvaged from another, similar bridge also destroyed. The idea was to make one useable bridge and rail connection out of two useless ones.

There were several experts in our group, one of them Imre Felder, a former top engineer of the Hungarian railroads. Enough bags of cement were found at an abandoned local building site. The necessary steel was salvaged from the second bridge.

Upon completion of the reconditioning of the bridge late one evening, we left the usual "CLOSED FOR TRAFFIC" and "DANGER KEEP OUT" signs all around the bridge and placed red lanterns on the rails at about 300 feet from the bridge in both directions.

Then in organized military formation we marched back to our quarters. Moving in military formation was the only reasonably safe manner of movement at night because, fearing Russian infiltration, the German and Hungarian military posts shot at all suspicious movement without warning.

During the middle of the night the ground shook, followed by a thunder-like noise. All of us, including the Hungarian guards, rushed out of the houses and gathered in a clearing. Everybody assumed that the Russians had moved up some large artillery and that more impacts would follow.

Our commanding officer, the captain, was on leave at that time and we were under the command of a first lieutenant whom we knew to be a much more humane and civilized person than the captain.

As it turned out within hours, it was very fortunate for us that he was in charge.

Suddenly voices reached us and shortly a few agitated peasants showed up. In the excited conversation, where everybody seemed to be talking at the same time, the only thing clearly understandable was that the bridge had collapsed. Without any orders, at least 100 Jewish workers and most of the Hungarian officers and soldier-guards started to move toward the bridge. From far away we saw fire and smoke. It was obvious that there was more to it and that the bridge had not just collapsed.

It became evident that a locomotive engineer pulling several freight cars had violated three red lanterns and stop signs and attempted to cross the bridge.

The consequences were self-evident. The concrete bridge-heads recently poured had not hardened adequately as yet and had given way under the load of the locomotive. The locomotive was partly in the water below. The rails were bent into fantastic twisted forms.

It turned out that the freight cars had been carrying German soldiers and equipment and the train commander, who appeared to be a top sergeant, had ordered the Hungarian locomotive engineer to pass the red warning lights.

Our Hungarian lieutenant called Imre Felder and after a short talk the two of them went to meet the German train commander. Everything happened within hearing distance and two things became obvious. Firstly, the Hungarian officer was not about to take the blame and secondly, that it was a clever decision to involve Imre in the discussion.

The lieutenant spoke nothing but Hungarian and Imre was not only an expert, but like most middle-class Hungarian Jews spoke German.

The German sergeant recognized our yellow arm-bands and knew that we were Jews. He was ranting and raving about sabotage, Jewish swines, that he would arrest us all. He even accused the Hungarians of obstructionism and treason.

Our lieutenant stood his ground and ---amusingly---, via his Jewish interpreter-- told the German that the Jews were under the command of the Hungarian Army and would stay that way. Additionally, he told the German sergeant that he would discuss the matter further only with a German officer.

At this point Imre had an inspirational idea and translated something that was not said.

"The lieutenant wants you to understand that if the matter is reported to higher German authorities he will make sure that it becomes known that you are responsible for the catastrophe because you ordered the engineer to drive through the red warning lights. The collapse of the bridge is your fault. Its construction was not finished and it could not carry the weight of the locomotive".

Imre looked at the lieutenant to indicate that he had "translated" everything.

The officer signaled and our Hungarian guards gave the commands and we marched back to quarters. I was walking next to the lieutenant and he looked at me smiling and said that it amazed him how many more German words it took to translate what he had said in only a few words of Hungarian.

As I said, we were very lucky that he was in command that day.

It is totally anticlimactic to say that as soon as German heavy equipment put the damaged locomotive back on the tracks we started to rebuild the bridge again.

DAVID AND GOLIATH
THIS "ROUND" GOES TO DAVID

The longest period in my "career" in Hungarian military labor service was spent in and near Komarom. This was the second time we were stationed in this area. It was also here that a small group of us, totally aware of the possible consequences, decided to risk everything and make a determined effort to sabotage the German war effort.

As usual, we were repairing and rebuilding railroad tracks. Our activities stretched about 15 kilometers east and west of the town of Komarom. They included important rail junctions and large marshaling yards.

Several Jewish forced labor brigades were added to our group. Since we were the only ones experienced in this type of work, some men in our brigade were put in charge of training groups of 20-30 men from other brigades. Our guard forces for the first time contained a few German non-commissioned officers and soldiers. All officers were Hungarian.

The sudden enlargement of the group and the combination of several work brigades into one unit resulted in the fact that the Hungarian guards were no longer dealing with familiar faces. We did not know the guards and they did not know us.

I became the leader of a group of about three dozen men. Our job was to maintain a running inventory of the quantities of all track-repair parts by location. We also had to distribute the parts physically, moving them by railroad cars, hand trucks (or on our backs if necessary) to the groups of Jews working at the various locations along the rail system.

Almost at once after the assignment of this job, we realized the strategic importance of it. We knew that we were in an excellent position to oversee the entire railroad repair activity and could make it succeed or fail, if we dared!

We were quartered in the empty rooms of a school and after a few days (with some friendly persuasion) we arranged for my small group to sleep in a corner near each other.

Our ambition and aim was to invent a method and effective action which would meaningfully undermine the Nazi war effort. After considering several means of sabotage, we agreed to pursue one plan. It had potential to be of really consequential importance but had the disadvantage that the preparation time could be long and the time of final execution was not under our control.

Our sabotage plan was to over-state intentionally the inventories on hand and to delay reporting shortages until it was too late to obtain replenishments. Our aim was to allow the inventories of railroad repair parts to be completely depleted. This would serve to bring the railroad reconstruction activity and the movement of German military traffic on the main line through Hungary toward the Eastern front to a complete stop or at least seriously interfere with its efficiency.

Our plan required making ourselves known to the engineers of the shunting locomotives and creating the impression that we had some authority, obviously derived from the fact that we worked for the German Transport Command. Toward this end, some of us walked through the railroad marshaling yard with clip-boards and appeared to be taking notes whenever a locomotive drove by. Further, we created piles of tools and hardware at strategically located sites within the yard, and whenever we saw a locomotive shunting freight cars, we took positions between the rails and held up our hands palm forward, the customary sign of a request for a stop. In almost all instances the locomotive stopped and we jumped up and told the engineer that we had military orders to take railroad repair materials to a certain switching tower. Occasionally the engineers refused. However, more often than not, they cooperated and stopped until we loaded the tools and parts into one of their, usually empty, freight cars. One of us jumped up on the steps of the locomotive to tell the engineer where the materials had to be unloaded. The rest of our crew traveled in the freight car. Since the movement of the parts served no purpose (except to create the impression that we represented authority), we always specified unloading destinations where we were likely to find another locomotive with which to exercise the same "performance".

In a couple of weeks this method of parts movements had worked itself in and we became "fixtures" in the yard. In fact, some of the engineers stopped on their own to ask where to take parts or equipment.

Our plan was working!

This is when we started phase two of our operation. Instead of moving small quantities of parts, we would move them by the car-load.

Usually there were plenty of freight cars standing alone or in pairs on semi-abandoned tracks. We examined the rail-switches and selected a freight car which was positioned in such a manner that it could be reached by a locomotive without difficulty. Then we loaded tools and equipment into this car. The next step was to stop a shunting locomotive and tell the engineer the contents of the particular car were needed at a certain location and we needed his help to get them there. This turned out to be easier than we expected. As hoped for, we established ourselves for the engineers as "genuine articles" and part of the "war effort". For the engineers this was only an insignificant change in their routine and most of them cooperated to the extent that they jumped off the engine to help us couple the freight cars to the locomotive they were driving.

We did, however, have a few tense moments. One was when an assistant station master came over, just as we were coupling a freight car to the locomotive, and asked the engineer why he was not doing the assignment he was given. I recall this as the moment when our careful psychological preparations paid off. " This is a routine operation. I am giving a hand to these fellows who work for the German transport command". The engineer's answer sounded completely plausible because he believed it!

In those days, and under the existing relationship between the Germans and the Hungarians, this was a statement which could not be questioned or contradicted. "Make sure you complete your check-list on time" said the station master and motioned toward the daily list of tasks which were posted inside all shunting locomotives, and walked away.

This incident made us think. We had to reinforce further the belief of the engineers and possibly also the yard masters and traffic supervisors that our activities were directed by the Germans rather than orchestrated by us.

Once the objective was defined, the details started to fall in place.

The germ of the idea was that the Hungarian rail personnel could not distinguish between German soldiers and Hungarian Jews dressed in German uniforms.

Almost all of us instantly thought of the Jewish tailor shop which was part of our regiment and occupied a few rooms in the school where most of us working on the railroad (including my small group) were quartered.

Upon arrival in Komarom the Hungarian officers were apparently instructed to set up a tailor shop of Jews to provide services for the Germans. Working as tailors promised to be easy sit-down work compared with the back-breaking job of building railroads. Obviously there were many Jewish volunteers. I assume that about ten percent were really tailors. About 20 were selected to become members of the tailor shop.

Two class rooms in the school where we were quartered were set aside for the "tailors". The Germans provided sewing machines and all types of supplies which they probably confiscated from the local Jewish population. At the beginning, the main activity was ironing and minor repairs and alterations. However, even for simple repairs, cloth was needed and the inventive Jewish tailors had a solution. They arranged with their customers, German officers and men, to provide old worn-out or ripped uniforms which would be used as material for the repairs. These old uniforms were stored in bundles in the tailor shop.

It was an obvious conclusion that the most believable way to prove to the Hungarian railroad personnel that we (and they) were helping the German war effort was to have them "see" Germans directing our activities.

We considered walking around in the marshaling yards, under some pretense, with one of our German guards. But this had so many "what if-s" that we threw out the idea.

Ultimately we all agreed that the original idea of some of us dressed in German uniforms, while exceedingly dangerous, was the only practical solution. The locomotive engineers and other Hungarian railroad personnel did not speak German and would not know the difference between a German soldier and a Hungarian Jew dressed in German uniform and speaking German. The danger of this plan was clear to us and for days we had trouble deciding whether to proceed. Getting caught in a German uniform was surely instant death. Ultimately, we never made a unanimous decision. The only reason we moved ahead was because four of us volunteered to put on the uniforms.

The process was not easy and it took a few days until we had smuggled three sets of German uniforms from the tailor shop to a little-used storage room located under a switching tower of the marshaling yards.

Again, our plan was to be implemented gradually. For our first test we selected a tall blond Jewish fellow, one of the four volunteers, because of his appearance and his good working knowledge of the German language.

One morning he walked a large circle to approach the switching tower from the back and walked into the store room, which was some steps below ground level. A few minutes later (to some of us it appeared like hours) he came out as a "German sergeant".

He joined us and we formed a small working group for our first "costumed rehearsal".

A small shunting locomotive pulling one freight car was approaching and stopped as we signaled. The "German sergeant" waved and gave the engineer a friendly smile. We loaded several cases of bolts, nuts and ties into the empty car. True to his role, the "German sergeant" stood stiff and looked on. As we finished, the "sergeant" jumped onto the locomotive and I followed. The "German" looked at me and recited in German the rehearsed text commanding where to unload. He also added some meaningless gibberish; I appeared to take careful notes on my clip-board. I told the engineer, in Hungarian, where the material was needed and that he should back into a particular siding for uncoupling the freight car to unload the supplies.

Due to the success of this "act", we staged several encounters between various locomotive engineers and Jews dressed as Germans. Once, unexpectedly, a yard-master was riding with us on the locomotive. In a perfect variation of the usual routine, our "German" friend jumped up onto the locomotive, shook the yard-master's hand and jumped off.

After a while all yard personnel (except one that I know of) was convinced that working with us was equivalent to working for the Germans. The one exception I mention was "Uncle John", an old yard-master. As he and I were walking along the tracks one day, he turned to me and said without any introduction: "I do not know what you are up to, but I wish you luck. If you need help, ask me". I swallowed and did not know how or whether to respond. I considered shaking his hand but realized that doing so might compromise him and our effort because we were within view of several people at the time. If he was "just testing" me, any response could kill us all. I just walked away.

Our activities were on schedule. We had established the hoped-for contacts and close working relationship with the Hungarian railroad personnel.

We now had to start concentrating on implementing our plan to run out of repair parts and hopefully to bring the railroad repair activity to a screeching halt.

According to our "master plan", I delayed as long as possible (as long as I dared) reporting to our Hungarian captain that we were running low on all types of hardware: ties, bolts, nuts and spikes.

The shortage became more important because, due to the extensive damage caused by Allied air attacks, additional Jewish laborers were added to the crew and were instructed to work day and night shifts. I convinced the captain that, since there was less yard work during the hours of darkness, it would be easier to determine inventories during the night shift. My group was detailed to work both days and nights and we moved into temporary quarters within the station.

We reached such a low point in inventories that "I had to come clean". In my daily reports I started to indicate that even after the most careful redistribution of hardware among the Jewish work details, we would run out of connecting strips, bolts and nuts soon.

The captain made phone calls and wrote letters, but because the situation was similar all along the line, as I expected and hoped for, he could not obtain any significant quantity of parts. A few days earlier I heard from a locomotive engineer that the Hungarian Railroad Administration was considering keeping only one of the double track lines between Vienna and Budapest repaired because of a shortage of repair parts.

After an emergency meeting of the German and Hungarian military with the railway administration, it was decided to salvage parts from branch lines serving local industry and grain elevators. We had not counted with this development. Luckily, it turned out to be a very poor source of parts because these were seldom-used and generally not maintained lines, and the rails as well as the hardware needed were practically rusted together. The teams which were sent out on this salvaging project came back almost empty handed!

One morning the captain told us his search had indicated that there were no available parts in Hungary and that a car-load of repair parts would be shipped from Germany. Most of us in my group, now between 30-40 men, instantly recognized this as the "opportunity" for the final action.

We concentrated our efforts on finding out the time and location of the arrival of the parts shipment. There were no published train schedules in those days, and German military and freight trains always had the right of way. It would have been possible to ask traffic clerks, but considering our plan it was not advisable to call attention to ourselves. Additionally, we found the traffic department had no information about transit beyond the Hungarian border. This was confirmed when one of us overheard the captain speaking with the station chief at the Hegyeshalom border station on the railroad field-telephone. Judging from the captain's side of the conversation, it was evident that the station master was of no assistance.

Considering the shortage of locomotives during the war and the flat terrain, it was a pretty safe bet that the freight car with our repair parts shipment in it would be part of a long train.

As we observed the actions at the marshaling yard they clearly indicated the expected arrival of a long train from Germany. Watching the activities of the shunting engines, which cleared at least ten tracks, it was obvious that the train, which was due in, was to be broken up into many sections. Since this was the only yard activity on lines coming from the west, we took it for granted that if our supplies were under way they would be part of this train.

We also noticed that at the same time other shunting engines were clearing tracks on the other, west-bound, side of the yard close to the main line. Red Cross cars were positioned on a nearby siding. Judging from experience, this meant the expected arrival of a German hospital train from the Russian front. This hospital train would be on route to Austria and Germany.

It was late afternoon when the anticipated freight train from Germany came to a stop on the expected track in the yard. We followed the train chief, at a respectable distance, on his way to the station- master. Their meeting was a reasonably long one confirming that the train would be broken up into several sections.

After about an hour, a yard-master came out and handed the job assignments to the waiting engineers of the shunting locomotives. In order to see what was transpiring without being obvious, we moved a few hundred feet away using measuring tapes and dictating meaningless numbers to each other. We had no real plan what to do next. It was clear that observing or following the engines was not a practical solution. We decided to approach the problem from the other end. We walked up to the train (and walking along it) took notes trying to look as official as possible. Our aim was to find the car with our supplies in it and try to convince the shunting engineer, who was to handle it, to drop it off on the other side of the terminal as close as possible to the tracks on which the hospital train was to arrive and later leave for Germany. It was likely that the parked Red Cross cars, probably loaded with medical supplies and equipment, were stationed where the middle of the anticipated hospital train was expected to be. Knowing that the locomotive would stop close to the water tower, it was fairly simple to figure out where the last car of the train might end up.

This is where we wanted to position our freight car with the supplies.

Since we did not want to talk about the hospital train, we agreed to refer to the closest landmark, switching tower #3 (with our German uniforms in the downstairs storage room).

We located the car with our supplies in it fairly easily because the name of our captain was crayoned near the destination tag. We surmised this was the work of the Hungarian station-master at the border with whom the captain had spoken, as described earlier.

Marshaling (redistributing) a train can be a very complex task and requires exact sequencing and timing, as well as the close cooperation of all engineers.

Total darkness was in our favor. After what appeared to be an endless period of pushing and pulling and coupling and uncoupling of cars and groups of cars, "our car" with the repair parts in it was alone, hanging on a shunting engine. While we stayed out of sight, one of my comrades, Jake, approached the engineer and asked him where he is to drop off the car. He said his routing sheet specified leaving it on a siding near the main station-building, where the offices of our commander and other offices were located. Since we "worked" with this engineer often, he knew Jake and was easily convinced that he should place the car near tower #3. My friend jumped up to keep the engineer company. The rest of us fitted well in the freight car.

It was past 10 p.m. when we reached our position at the tower and Jake jumped off the locomotive and uncoupled the car. The engineer, having finished a long day's work, drove off.

In the meantime, the hospital train had arrived and there was significant movement around it. However, since the platform was at the far side of the train, we were well hidden by the cars. We lay still for a while to discover the pattern of activity and to wait until it had slowed down. In the meantime, two of us carefully tracked down the rail-switches and found (fortunately) that both switches between our freight car and the hospital train were set in the "correct" direction. This eliminated the need to reset switches which might have activated signals on some control panel in a tower.

We had just about enough manpower to push our freight car and ended up a few hundred feet behind the last car of the hospital train. The train was already pulling some freight cars and, since all the activity was around the hospital cars, everything was quiet near the end of the train where the freight cars were located.

We pushed some more and coupled our freight car containing the railroad supplies to the hospital train going to Germany.

Our plan was completed!

There would surely be no railroad repair activity tomorrow, or until this car was located, hopefully far away, and sent back.

The slight banging of the cars of the train indicated that the locomotive had returned and been coupled on. The parts which would have made it possible to continue the repair of the damaged tracks were on route back to Germany.

We were sure that our action would result in a two or three day interruption in providing the German army on the Russian front with some essential supplies including ammunition.

We walked back to our temporary quarters in a barracks within the perimeter of the railroad station. There was no trace of the four Hungarian non-commissioned officers in charge of our gang. They had probably gone out to join female company for the night. We had observed this happening several times before and although we did not count on it we hoped for it.

Next morning all of us were searching (or appeared to have been searching) for the freight car. A Hungarian corporal called the station-master's office and they confirmed that the car with our supplies had arrived and was scheduled to be deposited near the Hungarian command office. There was no further confirmation available because the regular shift of the engineers had worked late the previous night and had half a day off.

Shortly after lunch, all Hungarian officers got together and made phone calls and started investigating.

They started to realize that the disappearance of the freight car with the repair parts in it made it impossible, or at least extremely complicated, to maintain the railroad tracks. A fatal blow to the German war effort. It was evident that the German Command would hold the Hungarian military responsible for the blunder.

Our commander, the Hungarian captain, understood there was no way out but to report the event to the German Transport Command. In a few minutes, several German officers and interpreters arrived and engaged in agitated conversation with the Hungarians.

After many dead ends, they questioned the engineer. He confirmed he had placed and left the car near switching tower #3. They did not ask him whether anybody else was involved and he did not volunteer any information. In any event, as a matter of caution on our part, he had only seen the one fellow, Jake, who had been riding with him in the locomotive. He did not see us getting into the freight car and we did not get out of it until long after he had left.

I have often recalled these days since and could never explain why we were not questioned thoroughly and even brutally (but this came later and with a vengeance)!! The only likely explanation is that our action was so incredible, unlikely and outrageous that none of the Hungarian officers dared to imagine it. Obviously, it was very helpful that the four soldiers on duty that night did not admit to dereliction of duty and firmly stated they had done a head-count at lights-out time and that nobody had left during the night because one of them was always on patrol.

Three or four days later, the freight car with the repair parts was located in Salzburg, Austria, which was the destination of the hospital train.

Instantly the picture fell into place for the investigating Germans and for our commander, the Hungarian captain. The engineer of the shunting locomotive was questioned again. The captain ordered my entire group to roll-call. The engineer was frightened and pointed out my friend Jake who, as a matter of total coincidence, had been riding with him on the locomotive. It could have been me or any one of us.

The captain commanded all available Hungarian soldiers to take positions behind us and ordered them to beat us with rifle butts. Most of us were lying on the ground and were still beaten. In some areas there was more blood on the ground than the earth could absorb and there were pools of blood all over.

It is a nightmare which still occasionally follows me. Lying on the ground, face down, on that sunny day and looking at the reflection of my face in my blood.

I can only partially recall the anti-Semitic ranting and raving of the captain, either because I was being beaten on the head or because I was so frightened out of my wits that my brain did not accept what my ears heard.

The consequences were immediate. Jake was taken into the switching tower and we heard several shots.

Jake died for a worthy cause, as one of the unknown heroes of the Jewish resistance!

All of us were surrounded by Hungarian guards and marched or carried several miles to the local German command post, which was located in an old fortress called CSILLAG (Star), and were turned over to the SS.

Even after fifty-plus years, I recall the sabotaging of the Nazi war machine at the marshaling yards of Komarom as the most meaningful act of my life.

After the war, the captain and the top sergeant who was the representative of the Hungarian "Arrow Cross" (Nazi) party in our brigade were condemned to death by a Hungarian Peoples' Court, and executed.

A VOYAGE TO THE UNKNOWN

My recollection of this period is (and always was) very hazy and spotty. I remember standing for endless periods in front of the gates of the prison. I recall marching around the prison, which only served to change places and to keep German soldiers busy. I remember running for food, but I do not believe that I recognized a single familiar face.

I had lost all my friends with whom I had spent the last few months and with whom we had risked our lives for a worthy cause.

I then found myself in a large semi-underground, cavernous room among hundreds of prisoners sitting or lying on straw. I knew that I was in the old fortress because the walls around the windows were at least three feet thick. As time passed, I realized that almost everybody around me spoke Hungarian and all the guards were German soldiers. When going to the washroom, I tried to concentrate on faces, but did not find a single familiar one.

The first people I talked to were Hungarian officers who were prisoners, which I did not understand. Then I found out the Chief of State of Hungary, Admiral Miklos Horthy had some days ago announced on Budapest radio that he ordered the withdrawal of the Hungarian troops from the Eastern front, terminated the alliance with Nazi Germany, and offered a separate peace to the Allied powers. These officers were members of his staff who were taken prisoners by the Germans immediately after Horthy's radio address.

One of the young officers was sitting next to me on the straw. He introduced himself as Lajos (Louis) Miklos, which at that point in time did not mean anything to me. Since he was wearing his uniform, I knew that he was a first lieutenant. Much later I found out he was the son of Field Marshal Bela Miklos (Dalnoki), who was the (former) commander of all Hungarian armies on the Russian front.

I saw a face I thought was familiar but it did not fit into these surroundings. Several days later, when my brain started to function better, I recognized him as Laszlo Bekeffy, a well known anti-Nazi stage personality, humorist, actor and friend and bridge partner of Admiral Horthy. Obviously, his connection with the Admiral as well as his well-known anti-Nazi attitude had resulted in his arrest. With him was a rather friendly person and I started to engage in conversation with him. He told me that he was Dr. Marton, a physician, and that he was Bekeffy's administrative assistant.

We continued to talk carefully and without saying much. One always had to be on guard because anybody could be an informer. An unusual coincidence gave us confidence in each other. During the small-talk, he asked me where I lived in Hungary. I gave the name of a small street in Budapest. To my surprise he said that he visited house #9 in that street very often. Since I happened to have lived in that house all my life, I asked whom he had visited and he named a lady well known to me and my family. I knew he was telling the truth. From that moment on until his death, Dr. Marton, Laszlo Bekeffy and I remained the best of friends.

Dr. Marton told me he knew some of the people around us and that they were members of Admiral Horthy's inner cabinet or household.

Bekeffy, whom I knew as an unbelievably humorous and witty stage personality, was a study in contrast. It appeared that his entire life was based on the false assumption that as a friend of Horthy he was not vulnerable to anything.

He was depressed, moody and a personification of Moliere's "Imaginary Invalid". Forever concerned, forever afraid, and most of the time "sick".

Dr. Marton and I attempted to assess our situation.

The guards were German, some SS. The Hungarian government was headed by the notorious Arrow Cross Nazi party. Both of them represented equal danger for us.

The only promising sign was that there had not been a single roll-call since either of us arrived. The jailers did not seem to care who was locked up. We did not know at the time that their least worry was bigger than us, because by then the Russian front was in the suburbs of Pest (the larger part of Budapest, on the Eastern bank of the Danube river).

About a week later, German soldiers appeared and chased us out to the yard of the prison. Only then did I notice that there were railroad tracks at the far end of the yard. On one of the tracks was an empty freight train, with all its doors open. These were the old World-War I freight cars, all of them still bearing the standard signs of mobilization for that war with the original military markings: "40 men or 8 horses".

The Germans set us up in wide rows of about eight abreast. We were directed to march in front of a field kitchen where all of us got a metal cup, a ladle of unrecognizable soup and a small slice of bread.

Then they marched us to the train and at each car they counted off about ten rows and commanded "up" and about 80 of us climbed into a car. It seems at one point they ran out of cars and pushed another 10-20 prisoners into each car. Then they locked the doors. We found the small windows near the top of the car were barred and boarded-up. The doors opened again and somebody reached in a bucket.

The car, designed about thirty years before for 40 soldiers (or eight horses), was so full with about 100 people that we could only stand pressed together without any chance of moving.

At first there was almost complete silence in the car. Later, small groups started to talk, some agitatedly, others just in whispers. All were equally frightened. The train started. We were in a moving prison.

After a while everybody wanted to be heard and everybody was talking loudly. There was only one subject. Where were they taking us? Even that late in the war Auschwitz was only a rumor, which most people liked to consider an unconfirmed rumor. However, it suddenly came up as a real possibility.

The mix of people in the car was diverse, Hungarian Army officers, former Hungarian Government officials, former members of the Hungarian Parliament, Jews with the yellow star of David on their chests and a few with the yellow arm-band indicating forced labor service in the Hungarian Army.

My sense of survival immediately reminded me that since there had never been a roll-call in the prison, the Germans probably did not know who was on the train. I assumed that being a prisoner of any sort was better than being a Jewish prisoner. With much tossing, twisting and turning I "wiggled" to the side of the car where I slowly removed my yellow arm-band and let it fall on the floor. Judging from the slot under the doors it was obvious it was dark outside.

We desperately tried to make observations to find out where the train was heading. Even if not the exact "where" we would have liked to find out the general direction. We made space for two fellows, one on each side of the car, to lie down and attempt to catch a glimpse of road signs or names of stations. Often we felt the train was crossing switches and knew that it was passing through stations. However, it seemed at all times our train was routed through secondary tracks far from the recognizable center of any station. Night became day and by noon we had collected only a few signs such as DANGER RAILROAD CROSSING, ATTENTION HIGH VOLTAGE or LOW CLEARANCE.

All signs were in Hungarian. This did not prove much, we could be moving east, south or west and still be in Hungary. East was not logical due to the proximity of the military operations there. We all suspected they were not taking us for recreation to Lake Balaton. This ruled out south. Most importantly, it also ruled out north, Slovakia, where the signs would not have been in Hungarian. This tended to eliminate the possibility we were heading in the direction of Poland and Auschwiz.

During the first one or two days everybody exercised maximum self control and did not use the bucket. We also hoped and waited in vain for the train to stop and the doors to open to let us out. Our hopes faded and during the third night the bucket started to be used more and more frequently. We placed the bucket under a boarded-up window where there was some air movement, but after a while the stench permeated the entire car and our nostrils.

The terrible conditions in the car proved to be a great equalizer. No longer were there top government officials, high ranking military officers and just plain Jews. We all became a bunch of miserable, hopeless and completely equal prisoners.

The train slowed to a stop and we started to hope at least for some fresh air and possibly water. However, it seemed from the clanking and bumping of the cars that either more cars were being added to the train, or the locomotive was being changed.

Voices coming from the outside were German.

The train moved on.

In about another day's time the train stopped without the normal rocking and bumping which would have indicated going through switches and changing tracks at or near a station. We were waiting for about an hour. Then we heard the clanking of hinges and rolling of doors and shortly one of our doors was opened. We saw German soldiers standing all along the train about a hundred meters away. A non-commissioned officer announced that we could get off the train, and instructed us to memorize the large number crayoned on the sides of each car to make sure that we returned to the same car. For most of us the most urgent thing was to relieve ourselves, which we did in a ditch not too far from the tracks. Judging from the behavior of the soldiers, this was the expected thing to do. This is also where we emptied our buckets.

We were commanded to form a double line and march toward a clearing where some burlap bags were piled up. A couple of German soldiers handed everybody a thick slice of dark bread. There were several large barrels and a few metal cups. Everybody drank from the same cups that were making the rounds.

This was the time when I picked up the Hungarian word --escape. Two young prisoners surveyed the horizon and as I slowly moved toward them started to hear enough of the whispered conversation to realize that they considered to make a run for it.

The train was stopped on a siding which at other times may have been used to collect and load the goods of the local farmers. Most of the German soldiers remained near the train, eating, talking laughing and smoking. Accompanying prisoners must have been a splendid assignment (surely better than freezing and being shot-at on the Russian front). They all seemed to have a good time.

They loudly called for one of the soldiers who accompanied us, probably to allow him to share in their good time. The soldier started to run toward the train.

The two prisoners contemplating escape took this as their clue and bolted.

Shots rang out and both of them fell to the ground.

Our feet were like clay or were frozen. Nobody moved, although probably all of us felt that we should at least attempt to find out whether any help was still possible.

We were instantly ordered to return to the train. There we noticed with shaking legs and voices that there was a destination sticker on all cars which had not been there before.

DACHAU 3 K

All of us knew what Dachau was, nobody knew what 3 K meant.

THE TRIP TO DACHAU

There was an immediate major change for the rest of the journey. The Germans removed the boards over the windows. The daylight and the almost fresh air in the car improved our mood and we looked toward the future with a little more hope. Little did we know this change in mood definitely influenced the lives of some of us. Several fellows had had the foresight to bring in a few wood sticks from the field hidden in their pants or sleeves.

Possibly it was only a subconscious recognition, but I thought that when I heard the German soldier close the door of our car and swung over the latching bar, he did not push the pin into place. If that was indeed the case and if the door could be moved slightly by just the thickness of my stick, I could possibly push the stick through under the latching bar and, by raising it, flip the bar back into the open position.

Almost everybody was watching or listening to what I was doing. I reached the bar several times and lifted it, but it always fell back into the locked position. Luck and the law of physics came to our help. Once as I lifted the bar to an almost vertical position, the train suddenly slowed down and the bar fell forward.

The door was open.

We were no longer locked in but nobody knew what to do with the sudden potential freedom. We were in Germany (Austria) and only a few of us, mostly Jews, spoke German well enough to understand and be understood, but none of us claimed to be able to sell himself as a "local".

The Hungarian officers were still in their uniforms, which we thought might create some sympathy in the old

Austrian generation, recalling the times of the Austro-Hungarian Monarchy, but it could be deadly with current German authorities, who considered Admiral Horthy and, by extension, his officers as traitors. Additionally, some Hungarian officers were dreaming of preferential treatment from the Germans (they were surely better than Jews!).

Most of us Jews, as usual, were victims of our infinite and entirely unjustified optimism. It seems that Jews, in general, were not contesting fate and waited for fate to come to them. I guess at this point in time I was one of those. As time went on my attitude changed significantly.

Four or five of the hundred in the car decided to jump.

After some time and discussion it was decided that late dusk and a rural area were the best conditions. It gave the Germans in the front car a reduced chance of observing, and it also decreased the chance of people working the fields seeing the movements. Those who decided to jump, or were considering doing so, changed clothing with others until all of them were wearing black or at least dark jackets and pants.

It was well after sunset, with only limited daylight remaining, when the train reached a rather sharp turn to the right which completely eliminated the observation of our car at the center of the train from the soldiers' car at the front. The train slowed down and six or seven people jumped. I was helping at the door and did not see the immediate results, but those at the windows said that all rolled off the embankment and gave the agreed-upon slight hand signal that they felt capable of walking. Only then did I realize that I did not even know the names of those who had jumped.

I hope that at least some of them reached home safely.

The train did not stop. There was no reaction. The Germans either did not see anything or they did not care.

Contrary to our first stop, which was in the middle of open fields, our train next stopped on a siding which appeared to be within an unoccupied military camp. The soldiers who opened the cars made no remark that the latch was unlocked.

We were ordered to march to a low barrack which had several long benches with a multitude of holes. Not very hygienic, but better than the last stop!

About one-half hour was allowed for just standing around the train. Each of us was given a slice of bread, then we were ordered back into the cars.

This was the first time it occurred to me to estimate the number of prisoners on the train. There were about twenty cars, I figured about 2000 people.

It was in the afternoon that the train slowed down and one of the fellows at a window uttered the fateful word: Dachau. The train moved through the station and kept moving. At one point, about 10-15 minutes after passing the station marked Dachau, the train slowed to a crawl, crossed several switches and came to a stop.

We were ordered out of the cars and jumped out faking non-existent energy. We often discussed the issue and it was our general opinion that the nazis wanted slave laborers and displaying strength indicates a possibly valuable worker.

The people who herded us were not the soldiers who had brought us here. There were a few SS men standing about, but most of the people ordering us around wore striped prison uniforms. As we found out later, these prisoners were the Kapos or trustees who did most of the disciplinary and dirty work for the Germans. We were herded on about half a mile. On my left was a water-filled ditch and a barbed-wire fence, which I later found out was charged with high-voltage electricity. Guard towers loomed in the dark. A building with a large wrought-iron gate appeared ahead. In the center of the gate were inset the infamous letters made familiar by every film, TV show, book or article dealing with the Holocaust:

ARBEIT MACHT FREI

(Work makes you free)

As we marched through the gate we were within the barbed-wire fence, we were in the concentration camp of Dachau.

THE GHOST TRAIN

The checking in of the prisoners even at that late stage of the war was an example of a systematic and orderly process.

I could and still cannot understand why the Nazis went through this charade when they knew that most of us would not get out alive.

All registration desks were manned by prisoner trustees, mostly Germans and Poles. The SS men and officers were circulating in the large room. I was in line and got close to one desk where they took personal data enabling me to overhear that one of the questions touched upon was nationality. I also realized I probably spoke better German than the trustee prisoner, likely Polish, who was asking the questions. I assumed that being German was probably the best of choices. When my turn came at the registration desk, I responded firmly, and somewhat unnaturally loud, that I was German and had been born in Oedenburg, which is the German name of the small town of Sopron in the extreme west of Hungary, with about equal Hungarian and ethnic German populations. I figured if it came to it, it would also explain my Hungarian accent. It appeared a good cover story unless I had to pull down my pants. The name Oedenburg I had to write myself, either to prove I was really German, or because the trustee at the desk could not spell it.

Our heads were shorn bald and we went through an ice cold shower, supposedly to be de-loused.

It was completely dark by the time we finished the registration process and were taken into various barracks in groups. The room where I was pushed in appeared to have been full of prisoners before we arrived. There were narrow passages between two and three-tier bunks partially covered by straw, and after the kapos had pressed back the prisoners already in the room we instinctively tried to occupy the available space. The number of bunks were so few that we were forced to lie cross-ways, seven people in two adjacent bunks.

A few days later, it appeared to be the middle of the night, when the room was suddenly called to attention. We jumped up and some Kapos counted off a large group of us near the door. In the darkness we marched to what appeared to be a stockroom and each of us was told to grab a broom. To my surprise we were led through the camp gate (ARBEIT MACHT FREI) and moved along the railroad tracks to an empty freight train. As we walked by the train, at each car the first four people in the column were ordered to jump up.

Our job was to clean the cars. The filth and smell was unbelievable and almost unbearable. It seemed these cars had served as lock-ups and transportation for an awful long time for a large number of people. Urine, feces, old soiled clothing, crumpled pieces of luggage, abandoned dentures and blood stains were the remaining witnesses of human abasement and suffering.

While we were sweeping the cars, flat-bed dumpsters were pulled along the cars by other prisoners and we emptied the contents of the cars into these conveyances. Other prisoners walked by the train and put into each car a container of what smelled strongly like antiseptic powder and several buckets of water. The intent was obvious. We were ordered to spray the powder on the floor and use the water to wet our brooms to clean the floor of the cars. In about an hour German soldiers and Kapos jumped up on the cars to inspect. In the car I was in, there remained a large area on a wall with what appeared to be dried blood. "You were told to clean" hollered the Kapo and kicked the prisoner standing nearest to him. He was an older person and fell forward from the kick. The German soldier stepped to the door and waved. Another container of cleaning powder and more buckets of water were reached in almost instantly. We got busy removing the blood stain while the German walked around and pointed out all other areas that still remained soiled and had to be cleaned better. By the time we finished the job, the cars were reasonably clean and the entire train smelled antiseptic.

From the direction of the front of the train a small group of SS men approached and again inspected the cars for cleanliness. They called the Kapos and instructed them to have us do some more cleaning here and there. They seemed to be compulsive about the cleanliness of the cars. When these inspectors were satisfied, our cleaning detail was moved to a platform about two tracks away.

The gate of the concentration camp opened and a group of hundreds of prisoners marched through and was stationed next to the train which we had just cleaned. The prisoners appeared to be in good spirits, in animated conversation, as if expecting something good to come. The sounds carried over sounded Polish to me, although I probably could not have distinguished among any of the Slavic languages. I noticed all the prisoners wore leather shoes and clean striped prisoner garb. Overhearing the remarks of many old-time prisoners around me, I learned this was a rare occurrence. The standard-issue shoes were slip-ins with wood soles with some textile straps. Leather shoes were given to Kapos and some prisoner functionaries such as physicians and administrative aids. Standing next to me was a man probably in his late thirties. He said he was a former officer of the Polish army taken prisoner shortly after Hitler's attack on Poland and he had been a prisoner in Dachau ever since. He told me he had never seen a large group of prisoners clothed as well as these. He introduced himself as Stan. He heard me speak German to others and spoke to me in very good German. He said he had listened to me and suspected I was not German. I was very concerned! How could I sell myself as German to Germans if I cant convince a Pole. "Are you Jewish?" I did not answer. "I have a good reason to help you and I will. Follow me". With that he turned away as if not to create suspicion by a long conversation.

The "happy" group of prisoners mounted the train.

We were directed to march to a brick building which was obviously an unused German military vehicle repair shop with several repair pits, but no tools visible.

We were kept in these quarters for some days and did general street cleaning work. The work took us long distances, mostly around military buildings, some several stories high, some single level.

It was then that I found out the concentration camp of Dachau was a relatively small area adjacent to a large SS military complex. The SS barracks were between the town of Dachau, visible in the not- too-far distance, and the concentration camp.

The rail connection ended in the SS military post and did not enter into the concentration camp.

The traffic I saw was exclusively military vehicles, trucks, troop carriers, and occasionally dark green or field-camouflaged Mercedes Benz cars. At times we saw other groups of prisoners, but we never had the opportunity to talk to anybody to find out what they were doing.

One morning we were not taken out for work. Judging from the greatly increased presence of SS soldiers around our building we all assumed that something was about to happen and were prepared for the worst.

There were two or three head-counts to make sure all of the work detail was present and we were kept standing as if to wait for an order, or a signal, or something.

The uncertainty of this time was frightening. Scanning the horizon, not too far off I saw a tall smoking chimney and thoughts of the Krematorium chilled me. My body shook. I found out later that the Krematorium was a much smaller building and what I saw was the chimney of the central power station heating the SS buildings.

After hours of standing in place, we started to move under heavy guard. We walked what seemed like miles along some empty railroad tracks in the general direction away from the gate, ARBEIT MACHT FREI.

As we marched on, we came to groups of freight cars parked on various tracks. At one point we were approaching about 15-20 cars and were made to stop. Most of the SS men who guarded us walked forward and formed two parallel lines on both sides of the train at a distance of about two to three hundred feet.

We were still standing in eerie silence and waited. It went unnoticed, but we were standing near a point where a kind of secondary highway crossed the tracks. Suddenly 6-8 large trucks showed up driven by German soldiers and took up stations near the train.

We were ordered to move up to the cars in groups of about 20-30. Standing near the cars SS soldiers and Kapos opened the doors. For a moment there was no sound, then a German on a bull-horn announced: "make way for the trucks, dump EVERYTHING into the trucks".

The EVERYTHING was hundreds of dead bodies all in leather shoes and striped prisoner uniforms.

This was the first, but definitely not the last time in Dachau that I had to handle corpses. It was difficult not to faint and I remember that I was throwing-up but still retained enough energy to keep going, to keep carrying.

It was obvious that this was the same group of prisoners we had seen boarding the train after we cleaned these very same cars a couple of days ago.

Several people fainted from the sight and the smell.

We never found out what killed all these prisoners.

Was their food poisoned?

Were they gassed?

Were they victims of some experiment?

There were a few bullet holes in the cars but definitely not enough for this mass murder and most of the bodies showed no wounds of any kind.

The bullets were probably meant to terrorize them, or to kill the ones who survived the systematic elimination.

What sense did it make to provide them with new leather shoes before killing them?

Why were they made to believe that they were on the way to a "good work assignment".

It was just the vicious lunatic game of cruel and sick minds.

A VISIT TO THE "KREMATORIUM"

It was dark by the time we got back near the concentration camp. We did not go through the gate (ARBEIT MACHT FREI) but were directed to march outside the fence partly on a dirt road and at times near brick buildings on a paved road to what appeared to be in the darkness a clearing in the woods.

On one side was a rather small building with a large chimney.

Dark and foul smelling smoke rose from the chimney.

We were at one of the most infamous buildings of the Second World War period: the Krematorium of Dachau concentration camp.

The march came to a halt. There was not a word uttered by anybody in our work detail. I believe all of us were too awe-struck even to be consciously afraid.

As I looked around I saw the clearing was surrounded by German uniforms and on one side several trucks were parked.

On both sides of the door of the Krematorium were large wooden bins.

A few prisoners came out of the Krematorium building and opened the rear gates of the trucks. The trucks were full of the dead bodies which we had transferred from the train to these trucks a few hours ago.

A Kapo appeared in the center of the clearing at the rear loading gates of the vehicles. We were told by the crudest and shortest of instructions to unload the trucks and line up the bodies in "single-file" one next to the other. By the time we had finished, almost half of the clearing was taken up by bodies lying on the ground.

"Remove all clothing and shoes and place them at the feet."

If anybody had any doubt about the identity of these bodies, the clothing and the leather shoes eliminated any question.

I heard the sound of a whip behind me. I moved around without stopping what I was doing and saw that a prisoner had fainted and a Kapo reacted by whipping him. Only moaning was the response. An SS man, even if not more compassionate, but cleverer and certainly more practical than the Kapo, shouted "water". Some cold water on the face and a bit to drink got the man on his feet.

"Bodies into these bins" was the next command.

Suddenly Stan, the former Polish officer, was next to me and grabbed a body under the armpits and motioned that I should pick up the feet. As we carried the body to the bin he whispered: "follow me when we get back to the camp. Nobody survives a Kommando (work detail) such as this."

Considering the speed and efficiency with which we worked, it is amazing in retrospect that by that time we were mentally so conditioned, terrified and brain-washed we not only reacted to commands like machines, but responded as if we wanted to please!!

As we carried the bodies to the bins near the door of the Krematorium, I was frightened to see that there were bodies at the bottoms of the bins as if "left-overs" after a day's work.

As the last task of the long day, we had to put all shoes, pants and jackets into three large piles.

It was dark by the time we marched through the camp gate. All German guards stayed outside the gate and we were guarded only by Kapos.

Remembering Stan's words, I did not take my eyes off him. We were in the middle of the group and I noticed he was gradually falling behind. I did my best to follow suit. When the group made a turn between barracks we were bringing up the rear behind the last Kapo walking next to the group.

Stan took off his cap, which I assumed was some kind of a signal, and moved sideways. I followed. In a few seconds a door at the far end of the barracks opened just about at the front of our marching group. Loud voices and conversation ensued between the prisoners in the doorway and the prisoners in the front few rows of the marching group. All Kapos ran forward, including the one marching just a few steps in front of us. We were near a set of steps leading up to a rear door. Stan threw himself to the ground in the small triangle of darkness formed by the steps. I was next to him in no time. There were no whistles or signals of any sort, the group marched on. As the sounds of the marching feet faded, the door above us opened and we moved in without straightening out.

Most of the subsequent conversation was in Polish and I did not understand anything. From the looks and sounds it appeared to me that many did not particularly care for Stan bringing me in. It seemed, however, that this group of prisoners were organized and behaved like military prisoners of war and some people had more authority to speak and to voice their opinion than others. Luckily, Stan's point of view prevailed, possibly due to his former military rank. He came to me after a while and told me that they would smuggle me over to one of the barracks used for sick prisoners, where I would have the best chance to survive. He explained I would have to spend a couple of days in their barracks until the transfer was arranged.

It was about at this time I started to feel sick. Mostly I laid on the floor in a corner. I had diarrhea and a throbbing headache. Stan looked at me and said: "You look green;

maybe our plan is better than we thought. You are coming down with something".

One early morning they told me to get ready. A short time later an ancient open truck stopped in front of the door. I followed Stan, who lowered the rear gate of the truck and, since I was dizzy and weak, he had to push me up. He was next to me in a moment and lifted the gate.

As we were lying on the bottom of the truck he turned to me and said without any introduction or explanation: "I am trying to save you in memory of my wife". I was sick and confused and did not respond.

The truck, which a few weeks later I saw every day, stopped at a barrack door and I found myself in a room with beds with blankets and with only one person per bed.

I have no recollection whatsoever of the next few weeks......

TRICKY CHOICE

You are through it. You have made it for now. Your temperature is near normal. I will try to arrange for you to recuperate here for a couple of weeks. Many people die in this stage after typhus.

Having said this, the young man introduced himself as Paul. He spoke to me in perfect Hungarian. After I responded automatically in Hungarian I caught myself. Why Hungarian? How did this fellow know that I was Hungarian? I asked him and he smiled. If you want to make believe that you are German I will not give you away. But for weeks you had a steady temperature well above 40 degrees (104 F) and people usually hallucinate in their mother-tongue, which in your case was Hungarian. After he had taken my temperature and pulse, he moved on.

It took me some time, I don't know whether hours or days, to try to organize my thoughts, try to figure out where I was, how I got here and where I was coming from. Even after that many questions remained unanswered in my mind.

There was no continuity whatsoever in the faces. Not the Hungarian railroad group, not the people in the train with whom I arrived in Dachau, not the prisoners dragging the bodies out of the ghost train. I gave up on trying to fill in the holes in my past. I knew that I was in Dachau and it was obvious that I was in what seemed to be a "sick-bay" or hospital ward. At the foot of all the beds were medical charts with diagnosis and fever chart.

Next morning a doctor, in striped prisoners' pants and a white coat, made his rounds accompanied by the young man who had spoken to me in Hungarian. They spoke in

German. The doctor's assistant asked me a few questions relating to my condition and illness, again in Hungarian. I thought it appropriate for the sake of the doctor and to try to reestablish my broken "cover" to respond in German (this incidentally was one of the facts that saved my life in Dachau). Standing next to my bed they discussed how long I should stay in the hospital ward. I recalled my days in the general prison barracks, the straw-covered bunks and seven people in two "beds". Staying in the sick-bay suddenly appeared extremely desirable.

I practiced German sentences in my head for hours to appear as fluent as possible for the doctor's next call.

The following visit by the doctor and his assistant consisted of a brief look at my chart. I responded in my best German to a few questions. I overheard a few remarks passing between them to the effect that I had apparently built up immunity to typhus and that I spoke German.

Later that day, or may be some days later, the doctor's Hungarian-speaking assistant came to my bed and told me in a very low voice that he would be transferred to an administrative job in another barracks of the prison hospital and that he had suggested to the doctor that I take his job in this room.

Nothing happened for days, when one morning the doctor came to my bed. "Get up, let me see how strong you are on your feet".

I had no idea of the purpose of this test, but understood that if I appeared well enough I might find myself without much delay in regular prisoners barracks. However, the same conditions would also qualify me for the assistant's job, which could save my life.

Having gone to the wash-room several times, I knew that my strength was returning, but how should I play it? Should I appear sick or well?

A FEW CIGARETTES
FOR A LIFE

After a few days on the job as the doctor's assistant (secretary) I found out that almost everybody in the room had pneumonia, diarrhea and either had or was suspected of having typhus. The infestation by lice and possibly the contamination of the water were the causes, according to Dr. Mueller.

However, the word typhus was not allowed to appear on the charts of the sick prisoners. Most commonly the diagnosis I was told to write on the charts was enteritis, enterocolitis, pneumonia or "under observation". On average five to six people died every day in our sick room alone. The cause of death was without exception: HEART FAILURE AND COLLAPSE OF CIRCULATION DUE TO ENTERITIS. ("Versagen von Herz und Kreislauf durch Enteritis") I do not know how medically valid or even possible such a diagnosis is, but since I wrote down the German version hundreds of times, I am sure that I am quoting it correctly.

I was instructed to leave the dead in their beds for a day and delay reporting all deaths one day later than when they occurred. In that manner the room always got a few extra rations of food (bread and soup) which were distributed according to Dr. Mueller's orders to those who still had a chance to benefit from some extra food.

I had a "sanitary assistant" who helped me to deal with the dead bodies. Since the vast majority of the people died after devastating diarrhea, typhus and typhoid fever and because the food was woefully inadequate, the bodies were only skin and bones and weighed on average probably 80-100 pounds. Handling them was a psychologically traumatic experience and not a physical chore.

The truck for the corpses ("LEICHENWAGEN") usually arrived every morning partially loaded. After a while I realized that the secret of keeping my sanity was not to look at the faces of the dead. I found this dreadful task of handling the dead easier if I adhered to this rule.

We piled the dead near the door and loaded them on the truck.

I recognized the driver and realized that on that fateful morning some weeks ago Stan had had me transported to the sick bay on this truck before it started its official duty of collecting corpses.

Since typhus was rampant in the camp, the dead were always replaced by sick prisoners. One such group included a familiar face and I identified the Hungarian lieutenant, my neighbor in the straw in the prison in Komarom. He noticed me as well and a sad smile crossed his face. He must have lost a lot of weight and looked really sick. I found a bed for him and told him that I would be back.

After I had done the rounds with Dr. Mueller and done my paper work, including the head-count report, I went back to my former prison-mate of Hungary, Louis Miklos. He had an obvious case of severe enteritis and considering his high temperature probably typhus.

The only medications available in the room were Aspirin, charcoal tablets and Tannalbin. The last two occasionally helped plain diarrhea, but were useless for typhus. Even these medications were continuously in short supply and never enough to satisfy the need.

Louis was too weak to talk. I gave him some Tannalbin and Aspirin and hoped for the best.

During next day's rounds Dr. Mueller examined Louis and took blood. Blood samples were picked up by a prisoner-messenger of the laboratory of the prison hospital on a regular schedule. Results of the tests were only occasionally received.

Dr. Mueller leaned to me and said on a low voice: "Typhus". Then he dictated loudly and officially: ENTERITIS.

Former lieutenant Louis Miklos of the Hungarian army was in our ward for several weeks and survived the typhus. On his road to recovery he told me that he was the son of field marshal Bela Miklos (Dalnoki), commander of all Hungarian troops on the Russian front. Louis was, of course, concerned that his father's top military rank and high position in the Horthy administration might result in special persecution by the Nazis.

I agreed with him that it might, but reminded him that when we were loaded into the cattle cars in Komarom, Hungary, nobody appeared to know who was who, and upon arrival in Dachau, the Germans showed no interest in locating any person in particular. At any rate the name Miklos is common in Hungary both as a first name and as a family name. Since Louis wisely never used the Hungarian nobility title "Dalnoki" he had an excellent chance of getting lost in the crowd. He laughed with relief.

Louis was in our sickbay almost until the liberation by the American troops on April 29, 1945. He thanked me repeatedly for saving his life and was weaving colorful rainbows of all the good things he and his family would do for me after the war. At no time did he ask anything about my background or my family. I did not volunteer any information.

I assigned him with the approval of Dr. Mueller semi-official jobs, which required the doctor to keep him on "sick" status. Most of the time he was cleaning beds and was providing bed-pans on request to the sick and washed those who could no longer do it themselves. All these may have been somewhat degrading to the son of the top Hungarian military officer, but he did it cheerfully, never complained and it kept him alive.

The existence of the hospital-barracks in Dachau was absurd, inane, ludicrous, farcical and for me totally inexplicable.

EXCEPT AS A COVER-UP FOR THE MEDICAL EXPERIMENTS.

There was no intent to heal anybody

There was no medication to help anybody.

No valid statistics were ever collected.

However, there is no question that the presence of the sick wards saved some lives, simply because they were less crowded than the regular prison barracks and they permitted some level of self-hygiene to exist. Because of this they were probably less infested by lice than other barracks.

I am sure, however, that this was neither the planned purpose nor an inadvertent oversight of the Nazis.

The reason might have been the intrinsically systematic and rigid nature of the German mind.

1--There must be a medical staff (even if it is of no use)

2--If people are sick, there must be sick-bays even if there is no medicine to cure anybody.

3--This is the system and there must be a system.

This brings me to the person of Hendryk, the pharmacist's assistant. He was a prisoner. If I recall correctly, he was Dutch.

I never found out where exactly the pharmacy was. Hendryk made his rounds regularly, maybe twice a week. Since we had no drugs and he had no drugs to dispense, his visits were mostly a confirmation of our needs. He spoke German and since he always appeared sympathetic to our cause, after a while I dropped my guard and became more open with him than I should have been and made reference to my history of Hungarian forced labor. I caught myself shortly after the fact and changed the subject.

All evening and half the night I attempted to rationalize that the Dutchman knew nothing about what was happening in Eastern Europe and my entire story had gone over his head, or was probably of no meaning or interest to him.

Luckily I mentioned it next day to Dr. Mueller and when he said that he would think about it and discuss it later, I really started to worry.

The issue was very simple and very deadly. If I was not a German, as was stated on the weekly sick room report, but a Hungarian Jew, I was falsifying records and, depending how deep the investigation went, I involved Dr. Mueller and his former assistant Paul.

There is nothing that we could do until we found out what Hendryk's follow-up actions or intentions were, Dr. Mueller said and continued:

"I know his boss, the pharmacist, he is not only a Nazi, but it is said that he had a leading Party position in Munich and was put into the camp because he was selling drugs on the black market. He would do anything that would help him get back into the good graces of the Nazi party. If Hendryk told him about you, you will be picked up by guards within hours or days".

Dr. Mueller continued: "Obviously in that case there is nothing we can do. But I think I know Hendryk, he is a rat, not a killer and I think he will invent something which gets the most advantage for himself".

One got hardened in the concentration camp by seeing all the dying and the dead and never knowing what the next day or text hour would bring. I thought I could or would never cry again, but the fact that Dr. Mueller always associated himself with me and always talked about "our" problem touched me deeply. Often I had to swallow hard to hold back my tears. He could have easily claimed ignorance of my true identity. What he really knew or did not know was meaningless, since it would have been his word against mine. There was little doubt that, based on his personal contacts with German doctors and several prison trustees, he would have carried the day. But for him it was always "us".

The danger of immediate drastic consequences appeared to decrease. No guards showed up to take me away and Dr. Mueller did not pick up any rumors during his rounds in other barracks of the prison hospital.

When Hendryk showed up the next time around we reviewed with him as usual our dire need for medicines, which was, of course, a pure formality. He knew that we had practically no medicines and we knew that we would not get any from the pharmacy. According to Dr. Mueller, they had a well stocked pharmacy, but obviously had orders not to distribute any medicines beyond barracks #5. We were barracks #15.

Barracks 1-5 were completely isolated and it was whispered that Nazi doctors performed "medical experiments" on prisoners there.

We were not allowed any contact whatsoever with these hospital barracks, which were continuously circled by SS guards. Once after I accompanied Dr. Mueller to block #11 I asked him about this. First he made believe that he had not heard me, or did not understand the question. Maybe he was just looking for the right answer. Then he said very deliberately and in a low voice, as if to emphasize the importance of his words. "I have no first hand knowledge. But <u>never</u> ask anybody. Knowing it, would not help. The less you know the better off you are." I appreciated his answer but somehow it created the impression that he did know a lot.

It was some time after the liberation by the Americans that it was confirmed that these were the death chambers of the SS human experiments.

During the meeting with Hendryk there was no trace of any consequence of my revelations to him. However, as he got up he turned to Dr. Mueller " Doctor, since you don't smoke and your assistant here does not smoke, you must have hoarded a lot of cigarettes over the years. (Doctors, trustees and assorted privileged prisoners had a weekly cigarette ration) What about sharing them with me?" The frightening part of the question was that it was not uttered as a question. It was a statement. It was blackmail.

However, I am sure that Dr. Mueller was almost as relieved as I was. If cigarettes were the price of his silence, I thought it was very cheap. As a non-smoker I had no idea of the value of cigarettes and did not know that they were a de-facto barter currency in the camp.

The doctor was thinking fast and carefully. Finally he told Hendryk to come back on his way back to the pharmacy. "I will see whether I can get some for you." With this answer he did not respond directly, he did not either confirm or deny that he had any cigarettes. Additionally, it was an unwritten law of the camp that in the event of any barter transaction you never gave away the location of your "goods".

As Hendryk moved on to continue his senseless round, I left Dr. Mueller's office, more a corner of the sick room partitioned by blankets, to give him privacy.

When Hendryk returned in a couple of hours, I purposely did not join them in the doctor's office. As a matter of fact, I made myself as inconspicuous as possible, bending down between the rows of beds as if counting blankets to be returned for disinfecting. They spent a few minutes in Dr. Mueller's office and I saw Hendryk leave. The doctor caught up with me a few minutes later and called me into his cubicle.

"The transaction was made, but I do not believe that the matter is over. I am sure this was only a down-payment and Hendryk will keep coming back. Incidentally, he also wants a pair of leather shoes."

Our source of shoes was entirely coincidental. Occasionally transports arrived in Dachau with prisoners (usually from other camps) who appeared to be very sick and were suspected of having typhus. These were not processed through the regular SS-administered registration process, for fear of spreading the disease, but were immediately sent to our sick-rooms located in block #15.

Since most of them subsequently died and because the corpses had to be put on the corpse truck (LEICHENWAGEN) naked, we occasionally ended up among other things with pretty good shoes. At that particular time we had three or four pairs of shoes in the small storage room and I asked the doctor what the next step was. Leave them there, I will let him pick, was his answer.

The shoes, however, were never picked up.

A new representative of the pharmacy showed up next week to make the rounds. Upon Dr. Mueller's question about Hendryk he said one single word: "TRANSFERRED". It was clear that showing any further interest could be a fatal mistake. It was also evident that the SS did not risk sending anybody who really knew anything.

Hendryk's fate remained unknown to me. I never saw him again either before or after the liberation of the camp. He might have known too much about the goings-on in the barracks of the SS "medical" experiments and been "eliminated".

MEETING AN OLD FRIEND

One day Dr. Mueller sent me over to the adjoining sick-room #1 in barracks #15 to borrow some blank charts.

A group of about 15-20 sick prisoners had just arrived in that room and was being processed.

In spite of his terrible loss of weight, I immediately recognized Tommy Deutsch, who was one of my partners in the railway sabotage action in Komarom. As I approached him, a sign of recognition lit up his face for a moment.

The almost yellow skin, the parched mouth, the hands shaking from fever were a tragic picture of typhus. I stood next to him not knowing what to say. He slowly turned to me and speaking Hungarian uttered " Pista (Hungarian for Steve) remember?"

"I surely do Tommy, and when we get home we will publish our experiences on how a few Jews confronted and successfully sabotaged the Nazi war machinery".

"You do Pista, I know I have typhus and I will not live to be there".

I tried to give him some support and cheer him up, saying that many survived typhus, that I had survived it and that he would get good care in this sick-room and would get well. After a few more words I had to leave.

On my return to my sick-room I told Dr. Mueller of the meeting and asked him whether we had any hidden medicine that may help. " Nothing that would be of any use" he responded.

"I will talk to Dr. Gruen about your friend".

The news was as expected. Tommy had typhus. Dr. Gruen gave him Aspirin and Tannalbin to try to control the fever and the diarrhea.

Next day I visited Tommy, he felt and looked a little better, his temperature was slightly lower. We whispered a little bit about old times in Komarom, when we thought that a small group of Jews could do something meaningful against the German war effort.

I left him feeling that he might get better.

Unfortunately I started to have abdominal cramps. Dr. Mueller assured me that this was really just enteritis, since I had only a low fever and because I had already had typhus and typhoid fever I should be immune to those. However, for a couple of days I took Tannalbin and charcoal tablets and stayed in our sick-room.

In a few days I felt well enough and went to visit Tommy.

There was another prisoner in his bed. Dr. Gruen told me that Tommy had died.

I spent the next week in total lethargy. I held myself responsible for his death. He might have pulled through, I thought, if I had given him the medication which I took for no serious reason. In spite of the repeated assurances by Dr. Mueller that nobody gets cured of typhus by any amount of Tannalbin, I was desolate.

Now, after more than fifty years, I still often think that I bear at least some responsibility for the death of Tommy Deutsch.

THE GAMBLE

A short time after Tommy's death we had an unexpected visit by an SS officer and a Polish trustee (Kapo). They said that they were assembling a work detail of about fifty to work outside the camp in the town of Dachau. The job was minor repairs, sorting and packing of German uniforms. Some knowledge of tailoring and German was required to prepare lists and read instructions.

Working outside the camp was the wishful thinking and the fulfillment of a desire of most inmates, especially if the job was as easy as this one was described as being. Plenty of volunteers stepped forward. I was tempted for just one moment before I remembered the warning of my predecessor Paul, assistant to Dr. Mueller. "Never volunteer for any work detail". At the same time a mental picture of the "ghost train" appeared before me. I also quickly realized two things. The first one was that I could hardly be offered a safer job in the concentration camp than the one which I had, and the second was the total lack of sense and logic of picking a work detail out of possibly contagiously ill prisoners.

I heard that the SS did not always rely on volunteers, but often just pointed at people to step forward. I kept slowly backing out of sight until I was behind a stack of blankets where I was as invisible as possible.

The work detail was assembled, the lists were made. Those who remained wished them good luck. The group left.

A couple of weeks later the driver of the "corpse truck" brought news of the group.

He had driven them out to a highway junction between Munich and Dachau where they were put to work cleaning up building rubble that was obstructing the junction.

About a week later he took out another group and brought back about a dozen bodies from the first group.

These prisoners were sick to begin with, and it was no wonder that they could not endure the fatiguing labor in the icy winter weather.

It was further unfortunate proof that my friend Paul was right. "DO NOT VOLUNTEER" because it is more than likely that you will trade your misfortune for something even worse.

INFORMATION GATHERING
(SPYING?)

Dr. Gruen, the prisoner-physician in sick-bay #1 of barracks #15, called me one day. We sat down in his small cubicle and although we had spoken several times before he found it necessary to introduce himself briefly.

He had a successful medical practice in Budapest and had been arrested on a trip to Vienna, where he had been invited to consult in a medical matter.

He ended up in Dachau.

We started to talk about Tommy Deutsch, my former comrade-in-arms in Komarom, Hungary, who had died in this room. Dr. Gruen related that Tommy had told him much about our sabotage of the German supply system in Hungary. He said that what he had heard was very revealing of my personality and that was the reason he had thought of me concerning the subject he wanted to discuss.

He was in contact with a Jewish work detail assigned to maintain SS command cars, including the vehicles assigned to: Obergruppenfuehrer, (lieutenant general) Oswald Pohl.

I admitted that the name did not mean anything to me. However I did know that the rank was that of a very top SS general.

Dr. Gruen explained that Pohl was one of the top SS officers in Germany, one of the advisors of Hitler and a personal friend of Himmler.

(See footnote #1 next page)

Dr. Gruen came to the point. The Jewish work detail, in addition to maintaining SS cars, had critical secret underground functions. Dr. Gruen knew some of the members of this group and was informed about their activities. He was told that an important Nazi-party-SS meeting was about to take place in Munich and top secret reports prepared by Pohl's staff would be presented there to Himmler.

The objective of the Jewish "mechanics" was photographing as many as possible of these documents and transmitting them to the Allied powers.

A small convoy of cars, including Pohl, would take the plans and associated documents from Dachau to a suburb of Munich, where they were to meet Himmler.

Pohl and his staff would spend the night in the SS compound where the meeting was to take place.

It was assumed that all non-coms. in Pohl's party would sleep in the enlisted barracks and all officers would occupy the guest rooms in the compound.

Himmler was to arrive next morning.

The outline of the plan would be discussed with Himmler.

After the meeting, Pohl and his staff would return to Dachau. The total distance of the trip was approx. 40 kilometers one way.

One of the cars in the convoy had a built-in security box and it was assumed by the Jewish work detail that the documents would be locked in this safe for transportation.

The safe was maintained, repaired and reconditioned by the Jews of the "command cars detail" and they knew the combination.

Footnote #1--After the war POHL was tried and condemned to death by the Nuremberg War Crimes Tribunal.: See APPENDIX

Photography of the documents required special lenses affixed to two plain Leica cameras. It also demanded the use of high-intensity lighting equipment. All this was available.

A critical question was where the car with the security box would be parked over-night in Munich. The probability was the garage in the SS compound. This would allow the use of lighting equipment because electric power was available and there were several storage rooms where the work could be done.

The final step was to pass on the films to the contact man in Munich for transmittal to the Allies. This was the only part about which Dr. Gruen knew nothing.

By the time Dr. Gruen got to this point, I must have had the world's most befuddled and confused face!!

He saw this and continued: "We need somebody who appears to be of military age, speaks German and has hair!!!!

I almost laughed at this last unique qualification, but then I understood.

Most prisoners had their heads shorn bald on a regular basis. It was an exception that some of those "permanently" assigned to work in the hospital barracks could keep their hair.

I had a full head of hair.

The Jewish "Command Cars Work Detail" was located in a building in the SS Camp containing a workshop and a garage area, where at any time several personnel carriers and other cars were maintained or just stored. One of those would be available for the job.

There would be four Jews in this car, the driver and three photographers, of whom I would be one.

The entire plan was based on the presumption that nobody would question the extra car in the convoy.

This was the obvious Achilles heel in the plan, but it was assumed that the involvement of Himmler and Pohl would make all the officers sufficiently nervous and preoccupied to take it for granted that the extra vehicle was somebody else's responsibility.

When I asked who the other three Jews were and how we would get out of the camp and to the SS motor pool, and how would I explain my absence to Dr. Mueller, Dr. Gruen knew that I had taken his bait.

The doctor responded as if he had forgotten a minor detail. "For the next few days Dr. Mueller is expected to be in barracks 11 where two physicians fell ill. I will oversee his room during that time". "But in any event I could handle it".

The good doctor had all the answers. He was no accidental middle man or innocent bystander.

He also explained that one of the prisoners was a young German. He was an inmate in Dachau because he had been hiding the fact that his mother was Jewish. The neighbors in his village had turned him in to the SA. His next station was the concentration camp.

The Kapo of the Jewish mechanics' work detail was part of the operation and would request four additional workers.

On the day of the action, the four (of us) would join the work detail in the morning and go with them to the workshop.

Since the workload of this group varied to satisfy the demands of the SS, it would not be unusual that the number of workers in the unit was four more.

Upon my questioning look, he assured me that this ploy had been tested several times and had worked. Naturally the SS guard kept track of the pluses and minuses of the head-count and they had to even out within a predetermined time.

From his discussions with Tommy Deutsch, Dr. Gruen knew that this type of challenge fitted my personality.

He was right, I agreed!

Everything went according to plan. The group of Jewish mechanics had several available vehicles and more than enough uniforms for all four of us. They said that vehicles brought in for repairs often contained complete sets of uniforms, which at times stayed around for weeks.

The final decision was that we should use a small Mercedes 170V rather than an open personnel carrier.

Exactly as scheduled, the SS drivers picked up the staff vehicles at the maintenance building and as the line of cars formed, we followed.

At one of the stops, the safe in the car was opened by two SS officers and a fancy red document container, emblazoned with gold SS insignias, was placed in the strongbox. The convoy was ready to roll. The first was a "lead car", small flags with SS symbols on the fenders, as was proper for the rank of an Obergruppenfuehrer. Then came Pohl's command car, followed by the staff cars, one of them with the safe in it. We closed the convoy. Our car was equipped with special end-of-convoy lights at the rear, as wisely prepared by the mechanics.

Upon arrival in Munich, Pohl and all the officers were dropped off in front of the appropriately guarded entrance of the SS camp. The area was cordoned off, obviously already prepared for the arrival of Himmler next morning.

The drivers took the cars into the SS garage and left for the enlisted barracks.

Unexpectedly, this became the most tension-filled moment as one of them asked us what our plans were. Hans, our German comrade, assured them that we would turn in after a couple of beers.

They really were not much interested and were looking forward to some female companionship in Munich.

David, the leader of our team, was sure that the officers had copies of the confidential document, probably each of them those parts which covered the areas of his specialty.

He also assumed that the original in the impressive red box (with swastikas on it in gold) would be removed from the safe shortly before next day's meeting to be handed to Himmler.

When I asked him how he dared to anticipate events with such apparent confidence, he responded with a single word: "Experience".

Obviously, this was not his first information- gathering action.

The photography went without problems, although when we looked at the volume of paper it became clear that we would have to use judgment what to photograph and what to skip.

We moved the high-intensity light, cameras, film, collapsible photo stands and some of the documents into a washroom.

David ordered that there should never be more documents in the washroom than could be photographed in five minutes. This was a preventive measure in case we had to interrupt our work quickly.

David was well prepared. He took out black (black-out) canvas folded into a small square from one of his pockets and blocked the single window. He also had several extension cords to plug in the lights.

The two cameras were working almost continuously. I only turned pages for photography and made sure that the documents already photographed got back to the red box exactly as they were originally placed.

One of the fellows was positioned as a look-out near the entrance of the main garage. His instructions were to warn us if anybody showed up anywhere on the huge vehicle parking area fronting the garage building.

Our lead-time, from warning until a person walking casually reached the garage, was less than five minutes. It was clear that this length of time was an absolute minimum to eliminate the traces of our activities and for us to hide behind some motor pool equipment.

There was one warning, but it turned out to be false alarm. It was an SS man who had eaten or drunk too much of something.

We wound up our work around 4 a.m. because we did not know when activities in the SS compound would start, especially due to the anticipated arrival of Himmler.

In any event, our plan was to make sure that we would be the first in the washroom. We hoped that the only remarks we would encounter, as the others started to come in, were that we were early risers.

During the early morning hours, two SS officers removed the red document container from the strong-box in the car and headed toward the main building where the meeting was to take place.

The SS drivers were sitting on a bench in front of the garage and waited for instructions.

A sewer cleaning truck showed up in front of the garage and proceeded to pump from a man-hole. One of the crew came into the garage and headed toward us. "A remarkable day for photography" he said, as if instead of good morning. David jumped out of the car and handed him a metal container with the films.

The man put it in his pocket and left the garage and joined the sewer cleaning team.

Our role of information collecting was done.

We waited in our vehicle for the meeting to come to an end. It was a fairly long wait.

Getting out of the SS compound was our immediate hurdle.

David had a plan and discussed it with Hans, our German comrade, while the two of them walked around in the garage.

Finally the drivers were notified, ran to their vehicles and started to move.

We were behind them.

They stopped before the first car got to the entrance of the main building. The reason for this became clear in a few minutes.

A large Mercedes pulled up to the entrance and Himmler, walking between two rows of SS soldiers, after much saluting and "Sieg Heils", got into the car.

The Mercedes left in a direction other than the main entrance where we came in and expected to leave.

It was our turn. Pohl and the officers got into the cars and we were on our way.

Nearing the gate, David and Hans jumped out of the car and ran forward.

Standing next to the two gate guards on each side they saluted rigidly and as the convoy went through they jumped back into our car.

It may not have been necessary, but I thought it was a good show!

In about an hour we entered the Dachau SS camp where the "Command Cars Work Detail" was stationed. We dropped away from the convoy and drove to the workshop.

That night, the head count of the work detail was plus four men, the same as in the morning. The SS guard at the ARBEIT MACHT FREI gate of the concentration camp noted that the four extra prisoners who left in the morning, returned to camp. Next morning I looked for the opportunity to talk to Dr. Gruen. The experiences of the past couple of days created the definite impression in me that I looked through the key-hole into an important information gathering network. I decided to ask Dr. Gruen what inside information he could give me.

We sat down in his small office and as soon as it became evident what I was going to talk about, he got up, put a bunch of patients' charts in my hand and motioned that I should follow him.

Prisoner physicians had the privilege of walking between the barracks containing their own sick rooms and were occasionally accompanied by their assistants.

Dr. Gruen got to the point immediately. "The 'Command Cars Work Detail' is the center for information gathering for the Allies. I do not know how the activity originated, however they are in a uniquely favorable position because of their daily contacts with high-ranking SS officers. Their activities extended from the simple tasks of keeping records of license plate and registration numbers of vehicles in the SS camp. This had given, or confirmed, information to the Allies of German troop locations and movements.

They were collecting names of SS officers and photographed all scraps of paper in the cars, or left in the pockets of their owners."

"It is amazing, but it is hard to believe, that an entire group of prisoners can act in concert as spies" was my answer.

"It is my understanding, and I do not claim to know all facets of the operation, that it started as an individual, or limited, action and developed into what it is today by careful selection of mechanics into the team. Some Kapos in the camp were involved and helped with assignments of prisoners with promising backgrounds and personalities.

"I do not know anything about their outside contacts, or channels of information flow", continued Dr. Gruen. "That is known only by a very limited number of operators." He then looked at me as if to indicate that the interview was over and said slowly and deliberately "In any activity of this nature one should be informed only if there is a 'need to know'. Be happy that you took part in an important operation, which may cause significant damage to the Nazi war effort".

We shook hands, and I felt proud.

THE PHONE CALL

One day I was told that some prisoners in the next barrack wanted to see me. They claimed to be my friends. My movement between buildings was severely restricted. I could only go if my services were required by Dr. Mueller and I accompanied him.

Also, moving around increased one's visibility and fading into the background was the most proven way to survive in Dachau.

After I received a second message, I talked to the doctor. He suggested contacting his former assistant, Paul, who had his office in the barracks from which the message had come, and asking him to find out who these people were. Since Paul spoke Hungarian (I found out later that he spoke about ten other languages fluently) he would be the ideal person to inquire.

The doctor met Paul and we received his response in a couple of days indicating that the contact was safe.

We decided to meet them after Dr. Mueller had made his rounds. As we approached the designated location, I instantly recognized my prison-mate from Komarom and on the train to Dachau, Hungarian stage personality, humorist, satirist, master of ceremonies and openly anti-Nazi, Laszlo Bekeffy. In the adjoining bed was Dr. Marton, Bekeffy's former private secretary.

They called me because they had heard that I had a responsible job in the next block and hoped that I would be able to help them by having them transferred to my sick room. They of course did not know that my job was entirely unofficial and depended totally on the good will of Dr. Mueller.

Dr. Marton looked seriously ill and his chart showed fever of between 40 and 41 degrees (approx. 103-104 degrees Fahrenheit) for almost the entire past week. This looked very much like typhus. Bekeffy had runny eyes and a bad cough with a lower fever. "I must discuss some very important confidential information with you, Pista, so that you can pass it on in case I die" Bekeffy said.

I vehemently disagreed that he would die, not only because I wanted to cheer him up, but because, indeed, he did not appear to be that sick.

A possible transfer depended entirely on the doctor of the sick room where they were and Dr. Mueller. Dr. Mueller was aware that an unusually high number of people had died in our room during the night and that we would have no problem finding beds for the two.

Since the unwritten law was that all typhus cases had to die in our barracks, a simple transfer could take place if the doctor in barracks #14 diagnosed both Bekeffy and Marton as terminal cases of typhus.

The two doctors walked away and agreed that the transfer should take place late in the afternoon, since occasionally doctors in supervisory positions made rounds during the early afternoon hours.

Shortly after the transfer took place, Bekeffy asked me where we could talk in complete privacy. The question was difficult to answer, since there was hardly any possibility of privacy in the large sick room full of beds. The doctor's partitioned off cubicle would have been available for me, but discussion there with a patient in the doctor's absence would have been much too conspicuous, which would have defeated the purpose. I tried to convince Bekeffy that most of the prisoners in this sick ward were much too ill to listen to conversations. Also, only a very few of them were from Hungary and spoke or understood Hungarian.

However, nothing convinced him. "You have to find a place where we can talk with the greatest confidentiality".

I started to be upset with him to the point that I hoped he would forget about the whole thing.

Fate gave me the opportunity to give it one more try. A patient died in a corner bed near the wall and I transferred Bekeffy into that bed. Some days later the adjoining bed became empty and I told Bekeffy that at the opportune time I would come by and we could talk.

The conversation took place next evening and it was mostly Bekeffy talking.

"By telling you this I am putting my life in your hands", started Bekeffy. "The only reason I am doing this because I think that neither Dr. Marton or I will survive Dachau. I remember well our talks in the train to Dachau. I recall that you know as much about me as a political humorist, satirist and master of ceremonies as anybody did in Budapest. You may have been wondering how I dared to be so consistently outspokenly anti-Nazi on the stage.

You may have even heard, since it was rumored widely, that I was a personal friend of Admiral Horthy, a relationship which protected me until the Regent himself was arrested by the Germans.

What you definitely did not know was that I was the Admiral's chief contact-agent with the British Government.

The reason I am telling you this is because I see that Dr. Marton, who is aware of all this, is even less likely to survive Dachau than I am.

There is no doubt and in my opinion there never was, that the Allied Powers will win the war and those who are still alive in Dachau at that time will be free. If I live, you have nothing to do. If I die before, you must make a telephone call in my behalf, regardless whether this camp is liberated by American, British or French troops.

You are to call a London number, In your first sentence, identify yourself and say that I instructed you to call and that I have died. Tell them that the papers are at location seven (7).

Nobody will answer the phone but you will have a definite indication that the line is open. You can speak any language, your call will be recorded and if necessary translated."

He asked me whether I would perform, as he put it, "a duty for democracy". I responded in the affirmative.

Then he gave me a telephone number and a simple mathematical algorithm which made the sequence of letters and numbers easy to commit to memory. He ended his statement by saying: "If I talk before my death try to keep people away"

I promised that I would, although I realized that this was a not a promise that was under my control to keep.

I also assured him that neither Dr. Mueller's last diagnosis nor his fever chart indicated that he had typhus and that we would both survive Dachau.

Dr. Marton, Bekeffy's friend, was the exact opposite of him. While Bekeffy always assumed that he had typhus and in general always assumed the worst, Dr. Marton insisted until almost his last moment that he only had a case of bronchitis, possibly a light case of pneumonia.

He died a few days after my talk with Bekeffy.

THE "NAZI GOLD"

As it had to, sooner or later, the day came when the option of volunteering was not given. A circular from the SS instructed several doctors, including Dr. Mueller, to give up the services of their assistants and make them available to perform urgent administrative work in the main reception building (the building where most new prisoner transports were processed into the camp).

The concentration camp of Dachau consisted of about 50 barracks arranged in two rows of about 20-30 barracks on each side of a main roadway.

We were to stand at the corner of our respective barracks at this center roadway at 7 a.m. next morning and wait for the SS to collect us.

Given what I knew about the fate of some special work details, it was more than justified that I was scared out of my wits. However, at this time there appeared no be no way out and if this was to be my end, it was so written in the book of my life. When I went to bed I started to pray silently, only to realize that I did not remember any Hebrew prayer completely or even reasonably. I prayed in Hungarian and really from the heart.

I might have slept some time between prayers, but at 6 a.m. when I got up it felt as if I had not slept at all.

Shortly before 7 a.m. I stepped out of room #2 of barracks #15 where I felt protected and almost safe and walked in front of room #1 to the corner of the building. Looking along the main street between the two rows of barracks I saw some prisoners waiting, like me, at the corners of their barracks.

In a few minutes an SS man and two trustee prisoners (Kapos) showed up at the front of the camp and came from the direction of the roll-call area (Appellplatz) toward the prisoners' barracks. The SS soldier stopped. The two trustees continued to walk between the buildings and shouted that we should join them on the double ("in Laufschritt"). About forty or fifty of us ran to the trustees and milled around for a few minutes before starting to march toward the main administration-reception building on the opposite side of the "Appellplatz".

Since we were not made to turn toward the main gate (ARBEIT MACHT FREI), the mood of this totally heterogeneous group, where nobody appeared to know anybody else, became somewhat improved. Incidentally, I was warned by Paul about such work-teams drawn from various barracks. Since there was no past association of the team members, one had to assume that anyone could be an informer.

We were herded into one of the large rooms in the reception processing building, where some prisoners were already working. There were eight or more rows of desks along the entire length of the room. Almost the whole center of the room was taken up by large wood crates of various sizes.

An SS officer standing in front of a large board commanded us to form a half circle around him. There were several types of official-looking printed forms tacked to the board. The officer explained that all desks and racks contained similar printed forms and our job was to collect all these forms and make orderly piles of identical forms. Once this was accomplished we were to work on the numbered forms and sort them according to serial numbers. We would be given further instructions once this was accomplished. He then added that we would stay in this building until the work was completed. Anybody caught stealing forms, or attempting to leave the building would be shot.

I overheard a few Hungarian words and joined those prisoners. Briefly we assessed the situation. The job looked very much like preparation for the transfer of documents or possibly as part of the evacuation, transfer or termination of the entire camp.

Depending on the nature of the documents which we ran into, we might not be intended to survive after completion of the job.

Most of our assumptions made on that first day turned out to be correct.

As we started to empty the racks and desk drawers we found a large variety of documents and selected some large crates and started to sort them into stacks.

In the top drawer of the desk that I started to work on was a stack of prisoners' passes valid for the town of Dachau. I assumed that these were used for trustee prisoners to be able to move between the camp and the town without being accompanied by SS soldiers. I noticed that the top few passes bore the official rubber stamp of approval. Apparently the German soldier or clerk had prepared a few more passes than were necessary. I knew that the potential power and value of such a pass was immense, but with soldiers and trustees circulating around I had no chance to hide one on my body. For a while I was undecided and kept handling other types of forms, but when I saw that other prisoners were getting near I decided to make a move.

The two Hungarian Jews, Peter and Andy, whom I had met in the morning during the march to the administration building were working close together. Carrying a large stack of documents I walked by them and whispered to them to follow me. As we moved together, all three of us loaded with blank forms, I told them that I had found papers valuable for all of us and that they must create some diversion to allow me to pocket them.

Their execution was simple and perfect. They instantly recognized which trustee was near the desk which I pointed out and as soon as they saw me getting back to the desk, they started to push around a creaky old desk about ten desks away from me. They cursed loudly that a drawer was stuck and they could not open it unless they lifted one side. The trustee moved there rapidly as expected. By the time he got there the drawer was amazingly open and I had the papers in my pocket.

After the day's work we were herded to our night quarters. As we moved through a corridor into the room we walked by a guard area with gun-rack, and two small tables and chairs. At that moment two SS soldiers were playing cards. Behind in the corridor there were three doors, one, with two zeros indicating a lavatory. The other larger, locked, door was without any marking. At the end of the corridor, as a continuation of it, was a set of open double doors into the room which would become our quarters. Except for a few long benches it was empty.

No German soldier or trustee came in with us into the room. I guess there was nothing to instruct. It was clear that we were to sleep on the floor. The benches were stacked on one another. Some people pulled them apart and sat on them. Andy, Peter and I figured that it was more important to secure a private corner for the night and sat on the floor in a corner of the room.

Most prisoners spoke German or Slavic languages. We heard no Hungarian spoken. However, we had to be careful because any group of people talking German might have consisted of diverse nationalities (including Hungarian) who used German as a common language. The three of us dropped some carefully chosen words which were hope-

As these choices and possibilities rushed through my head and also possibly the doctor's mind, he reached out his hand "I am Dr. Mueller" he said. This was an obvious sign. (I did not assume that it was a trick). Why would he introduce himself if he wanted to transfer me out? When I got out of bed, I put the best possible spring into my steps that I could muster.

He turned to me and smiled. "Paul will bring you some clothes later and we will make our rounds together tomorrow morning. You speak German and your blood tests show that you have survived typhus and typhoid fever. Both your Gruber-Widal and Weil-Felix tests were positive. You should have built up the immunity necessary to stay alive in this room. You can carry on Paul's duties after he leaves to take on another job".

Later Paul dropped off on my bed some poor but clean clothing smelling strongly of disinfectant. He came close to my head and almost whispered: "I will be transferred to another barracks in a few days. I want to leave you one piece of advice: Never volunteer for any special work detail. Try to stick with Dr. Mueller, that is your best bet.

fully meaningless to anybody else. Between half-finished sentences we came to the conclusion that the papers could be examined and change hands only in the lavatory.

Peter went through the open double doors of our room to check out the bathroom. When he came back he reported that there were three booths and the standard German circular military wash basin with several faucets. He also tried the door on the other side of the corridor. He said that it was locked, but it was an ill-fitting door. We, of course, had no idea where this door lead to, or what to do with this knowledge.

We decided that whoever woke up at night would wake up the other two and that Andy and Peter would follow me one by one to the bathroom .

After lights-out I lay awake for a long time and noticed some light spilling over from around the bend in the corridor where the guards were and also saw a narrow weak slit of light under the door of the wash room.

One of the prisoners got up and went to the bathroom. As he closed the door on his way back, a German soldier became visible for a moment at the bend of the corridor. Apparently satisfied, he went back to the guard station.

All was quiet for quite a while and I thought that this time was as good as any and I nudged Andy and Peter and started to the bathroom. It was empty.

Andy and Peter came in shortly and without wasting time I gave them each, one stamped official pass for "Unaccompanied Prisoner to the Town of Dachau". They put the unfolded paper under their shirts.

We would now wait for the opportunity to use them.

The work continued next day and it seemed that there was no end to the kind and quantity of forms generated by the German bureaucracy.

As we continued, Andy showed up next to me and whispered the word "keys". I had no idea what he meant, or what it was all about, but in a little while I walked by the desk he was emptying and we acted as if to combine some stacks of forms.

He bent down and carefully and silently put a bunch of keys, which he had obviously found in a desk drawer, on the floor. Then it came to me. His prison garb had no pockets and since my hospital coat had pockets he wanted me to pick up and hide the keys.

I dropped a bundle of papers, bent down, picked up the keys together with the papers and walked back to my station.

As we worked our way across the large reception room we reached two metal cabinets. Both had two pairs of hinges and padlocks. Clearly they served other purposes than the storage of office supplies.

As some of us gathered curiously around the cabinets, the trustees gave instant orders to us to step back and one of them ran to the SS office for instructions. The issue appeared to be too complicated to allow an immediate answer and an SS officer made us put the cabinets close to each other and set up benches around them. In a short while he came up with hand-written paper signs, "ACHTUNG" "do not handle", which he glued on the fronts of the two cabinets.

We continued with our usual work, but most of us were hatching theories as to what the two cabinets could contain. The only things we knew for sure was that they were well secured and were very heavy.

The day passed and as we returned to our quarters for the night we found piles of old German army blankets on the floor. To most of us this was a good sign. It appeared to mean that the Germans planned additional work for us in this building and gaining time in Dachau held the possibility of gaining life.

During our discussion of this and our chances of survival in general, Andy suddenly changed the subject and told me that he wanted to examine the keys that he had found. He said that he would nudge me during the night to pass to him the batch of keys which I kept in my pocket wrapped in toilet paper. He said that he wanted to take a close look to determine whether they might be keys for padlocks (he was thinking of the two metal cabinets).

I found out in subsequent conversations that he had worked in his father's hardware store and had years of experience as a locksmith's apprentice.

I made sure that the keys were tightly wrapped so that they would make no noise, lay down on the floor and pulled the cover over me.

It was not much after lights-out and I was still awake and thinking, when Andy signaled and I put the keys in his extended hand. After a few minutes, he slowly raised himself and headed for the wash room. I did not have to wait long, he was back in a short while and lying down put the keys in my hand.

Next morning while washing, he said "Looks possible, but must look at the locks."

But how?

The chance presented itself faster than we expected.

As we moved into the work area we were assembled in a corner and an SS officer made the announcement that the first task this morning would be to move the two steel cabinets. He said that the tools were already available at a rear entrance and that he would select ten of us to do the job. Andy thought fast. Since this type of selection was usually from those standing in the front he instantly started to worm his way between people toward the front. By the time the

SS officer had commanded and motioned that that ten prisoners should step forward, Andy was in the first row and happily stepped forward. More than ten prisoners moved forward and the SS man rounded them down, but Andy remained as one of the ten.

The ten were set up in double file and were commanded to march under the supervision of two Kapos. They returned shortly with some furniture-movers' levers, crow bars, rope and other tools.

In order to move the cabinets in the designated direction several desks had to be moved to clear a wide path to the door. The door led to the corridor to our night-quarters as well as toward the locked entrance door of the unknown area. This made the destination of the steel cabinets evident. The only question was whether or not the room or rooms behind the locked door had an exit to the outside.

Working around and moving the cabinets gave Andy the opportunity to take a close look at the padlocks.

The steel cabinets turned out to be extremely heavy. It required about six people to push the levers and to balance the cabinets side-ways. However, the transfer went without a hitch. It was probably this that gave the SS officer in command the charitable idea of allowing us a half hour of fresh air behind the building. It was cold but we enjoyed it thoroughly, especially because there was no compulsory gymnastics involved. We just milled around and talked.

Andy reported that several of the keys were definitely the types which could fit the locks. He also noted that the room into which the steel cabinets had been moved was full of electrical materials and equipment possibly repair and spare parts for the high-voltage electrical fence which surrounded the concentration camp. He also saw that there were large double sliding doors leading to an exterior loading ramp.

It was clear to us that any attempt to get near the cabinets would involve serious danger and that if we were caught trying to open them we might pay with our lives.

Our desire to do it was inflamed by the obvious importance and the secrecy which the SS attached to these cabinets.

Furthermore, all three of us were about twenty years old, old enough to understand fully the tragic fate of the Jews in Hitler's "FINAL SOLUTION", but young enough to think that individual actions might still make a difference. However, more than anything else, we wanted to be in a position, if we survived, of being able to bear witness and talk about the inside workings of Dachau concentration camp as a workshop of the "FINAL SOLUTION".

We decided to try, actually Andy decided to try, since he was the only one who could judge whether the keys were even close to fitting.

At this time we did not get any further than deciding to try. We had no plan except to look for opportunities.

To our surprise, we found out that when picking up the tools to move the cabinets Andy had spotted a tool tray on the truck and while everybody was busy otherwise, he quickly broke a small needle file in half and squeezed it into his shoes. He had it there in various positions ever afterwards. The file would give him the chance to make minor modifications to a key that almost fitted.

Our work routine changed after the cabinets had been moved into the electrical stockroom. Every day four or five SS men spent hours in the room behind closed door.

Then one morning about half a dozen of us were sent into the room for a general clean-up, including cleaning the windows. I was in the cleaning detail, but Peter and Andy, with most of the other fellows, continued with the job of sorting and packaging documents.

On the second day of cleaning we overheard the SS guards discussing that an inspection by high-ranking military was expected.

Hence the extraordinary clean-up.

My first thought was that it might promote our plans to change places with Andy, but I realized that we were almost an equal number of prisoners and SS soldiers in the room and there would be no opportunity to even get close to the cabinets, especially since the SS placed tables and benches around the cabinets. They used these tables to spread out some ledgers on which they were working.

An SS officer showed up in the room and, after marching up and down a few times, expressed loudly and with much vulgarity his total dissatisfaction with the cleaning. It seems that he really wanted to impress the visitors with a "showcase" presentation.

As he was leaving, he turned back to our SS guards, who, of course marched behind him during his inspection, and warned: "You had better invent something and do better than this".

The SS guards looked at each other in helpless amazement.

It was clear that it was only a question of time before they would vent their wrath on us.

At this point in time I had an inspired idea and a plan.

I walked over to the guards and, appearing totally helpful, suggested that they get some paint and brushes and we paint the window frames, the entrance door, the sliding doors of the loading dock and the floor of the loading platform.

Painting before an inspection is the most common and popular action in probably any army in the world.

The response was a single word from the sergeant "Fantastisch!" (fantastic!).

After a short talk among the SS, the sergeant told me to follow him with two men.

Within the hour, gallons of German military gray paint, brushes of all sizes and small tools were in the room at strategic locations.

Since the painting was my idea, the sergeant happily said "Tell them what to do".

I did not want to play my hand right away and organized the little group to paint window frames and the sliding doors of the loading dock.

At night I shared my plan with Andy and Peter. The aim was to start painting the entrance door and the door frame next morning. I would try to persuade the SS that we could do a better job if we unhinged the door. However, whether or not we took the door off its hinges, the paint would be still wet in the evening and the door would have to stay open.

This, at least, was the plan.

At that point any further action (if any) to get to the cabinets during the night depended on whether the SS would agree not to hang the door back on it's hinges and if they agreed, the precautions which the they would take in guarding the open door.

I was so excited that I could hardly sleep all night and noticed that Andy and Peter also kept twisting and turning under their covers.

Next day everything went according to plan and the sergeant's resolve was fortified by the officer who came to inspect and expressed his satisfaction about the painting idea, while probably congratulating himself on his efficient approach to command.

My proposal to take the door off its hinges to allow for a better paint job was approved by the SS without comment.

At quitting time, as expected, the paint on the door and on the frames was still wet and the SS decided to block the entrance by two desks one on top of the other.

On their way out they stopped at the guard station and came back with one of the guards on duty. They talked together for quite some time in front of the blocked entrance.

The evening head-count was in the main registration room and that is where I caught up with Andy and Peter and brought them up to date. All planning and preparations that we could do were done.

On the way back to our night quarters there was no guard at the blocked door.

We went back to our room and sat in our corner. Through our open door, from Peter's position he could just see the blocked entrance. We bunched up together and watched and waited.

After a while it became clear what we were up against. One of the guards from the guard station walked by the door every half hour. He reached for the switch, turned on the light, looked in, turned off the light and went back to the guard station.

There was usually fairly frequent traffic to the bathroom after lights-out so we waited about an hour and followed each other (barefoot) to the wash room. We decided that Peter should be the last one and come exactly after the guard had made his round and disappeared around the corner on his way back to the guard station. This would give us the maximum time to examine the cabinets.

We were ready as he stepped into the wash-room. Since we would be visible and recognizable from the prisoners' room when we crossed the corridor, we decided on the risk of turning off the bathroom light.

All went fast. In a few seconds we were past the desks blocking the door and they followed me to the cabinets.

Andy instantly and silently started to work with the keys. He had to work essentially by feel because the only light we had was provided by a small black-out lamp outside under the roof of the loading dock. We practically held our breaths and waited for Andy to turn his magic. It was at this time that we realized that if Andy had to use his file to modify a key the noise would surely give us away. Our hopes rose after we heard the first faint click. The second followed shortly.

Clearly, the SS man who had left his keys in the desk drawer must have been in charge of these very cabinets.

We were frightened to death by a sudden increase of light, but it was only a prisoner who had turned the light back on in the wash room.

Very gently Andy opened the door of the cabinet.

Its shelves were full of boxes carefully numbered and dated. Reaching into one box revealed gold rings, chains, bracelets and other jewelry. Another box was full of gold coins, most of them recognizable even in the darkness as "Maria Theresa Thalers" which were the standard barter currency of European Jews.

We did not even recognize at first what we held in our hands when we reached into some other boxes. They were gold crowns and gold fillings from teeth. We opened and reached into several boxes in the cabinet and found that more than half of them contained gold teeth.

There must have been tens of thousands of them.

I shivered when for a moment as I allowed a mental picture to form about the origin of these teeth.

It was about 50 years later that the civilized world realized with dismay, revulsion and horror that some Nazi gold bars in the vaults of Swiss banks might contain gold from these very teeth!!

(See footnote #2)

We heard the guard coming. Peter and I ducked behind the desks. Andy, with great presence of mind, quietly closed the door of the cabinet and stepped behind it.

The guard went through his routine and left.

Without saying a word, we were elated. With good planning, youthful bravery and much luck we had achieved what we had set out to do.

Andy locked the cabinet and one by one we sneaked back to the washroom and from there to our quarters and under the covers.

Next day I continued the paint job with my crew, Peter and Andy went to their jobs of sorting documents.

I found Andy's small broken file on the floor near the cabinet and dumped it in a can of paint.

Obviously we were not present at the inspection, but we saw the very high ranking SS officers go through the building.

It was a dark cloudy morning; looking through the windows of the reception room, where we still sorted SS documents, we observed unusual military activity. At the north perimeter of the APPELLPLATZ hundreds of German soldiers were lining up at arms-length three or four men deep. The view to the low silhouette barracks of the concentration camp, located behind the rows of soldiers, was almost totally obstructed.

Footnote # 2

Articles about the **"Nazi Gold"** started to appear in THE NEW YORK TIMES in May of 1997. This was 53 years after we discovered and held in our hands probably close to 1000 pounds of gold, including gold teeth, crowns and fillings, apparently removed by the Nazis from the bodies of their victims.

See Appendix

One of the unusual part of the operation was that the main gate of the camp was wide open which made the mocking aphorism of "ARBEIT MACHT FREI", inserted into the gate, not visible.

We kept walking by the windows to "sneak a peek", and to find out what was happening, but everything appeared like a still, frozen picture. There was no movement.

A while later we heard noises and saw two civilian armored cars, such as those carrying money to and from banks, entering the camp. Each had two men in the driver's compartment and one SS soldier riding on the running board on each side of the drivers' cabins.

The view presented to these civilian drivers, if they were interested at all, was no different than entering any military camp.

The armored cars stopped at the loading platform of the administration/reception building and several soldiers loaded the two metal cabinets containing the **"Nazi Gold"** one into each car.

During the entire operation the soldiers riding on the running boards of the armored cars did not move and gave no opportunity for the drivers to get out of the vehicles.

Upon completion of the loading the cars left without delay followed by an SS military vehicle with four soldiers in it. The main gate was closed and the ARBEIT MACHT FREI became visible again. Within minutes the hundreds of soldiers, having accomplished their task of obscuring the view to the concentration camp, marched out of the camp.

The "show" arranged by the SS to provide a pretty transparent cover for the "laundering" of the financial remnants of millions of Jews who perished by their bloody hands, was over.

We witnessed the transfer of the **"Nazi Gold"** from the SS to German civilian authorities, (REICHSBANK?) for melting it into gold bars thus eliminating all traces of the source.

It is more than amazing that it took over 50 years for these facts to surface, considering that they must have been known to, or suspected by, thousands of people at the time they actually took place.

DECEIVING THE RED CROSS

Our document-sorting job ended with loading the crates into which we had packed the documents onto trucks.

At the last roll call, all of us got a pass indicating the number of the barracks from which we had come and to which we must return.

Since for some reason we were divided into several groups during the roll-call, I lost contact with Andy and Peter. I never saw them again before or after the liberation.

I wonder whether they tried to make use of the passes to Dachau town which I gave them. As a graver matter, I never found out whether they survived.

Leaving the administration building, we crossed the "Apellplatz" in military formation and were then told to continue on our own to our designated barracks. This was most unusual, since unaccompanied prisoners were a rare sight in Dachau. The exceptions were trustee prisoners (Kapos) doctors, electricians, plumbers and construction workers.

As I was marching toward "Block" (barracks) #15 in the cold winter morning I started to hear noises coming from behind me. As I carefully tuned my head I saw that the noise was coming from the main gate (ARBEIT MACHT FREI) of the camp. I saw SS and Kapos milling around. I did not dare to stop and look, but slowed down and turned into a narrow corridor between two barracks where I could look back without making my presence obvious and where I dared to stop. Shouting, cursing and general turmoil was evident. A little later the sound of whiplashes could be heard.

From words and fractions of sentences it became clear that the SS and some Kapos were bringing back a prisoner who attempted to escape. The prisoner had to repeatedly shout the words: "Ich bin wieder da" (I am back again)

Every so often the Kapos made the unfortunate soul stop and occasionally two of them simultaneously whipped him.

It was his crying that got me out of my stupor and made me realize that this was no time to be a witness. Turning into the corridor between barracks was an unbelievably stupid idea because it was not on the way to my destination and if anybody stopped me I could not explain my presence. I guess I got carried away by my desire to find out and forgot about doing everything to be reasonably safe. I quickly got back to the main drag on the way to Block #15 and speeded up. At the same time I knew that probably the most dangerous thing I could do was to run. So I attempted to discipline myself and moved on at a brisk but controlled

The sounds of crying became softer, not because I got pace. much farther from the scene, but because the prisoner was near exhaustion and was just stumbling forward. He was on the verge of passing out. This also ended the "fun" for the Kapos and their cruelty became less enthusiastic.

As I neared Block #15 frightening thoughts engulfed me.

What if my job had been taken by somebody else?

What if Dr. Mueller was no longer in charge of this sick-room?

What if this was only a temporary address to come back to and I had to go to a new work assignment?

As I walked through the door of the sick-room, I was afraid to raise my head and turned toward Dr. Mueller's cubicle, without looking.

I instantly heard him calling me from the other end of the room. "Glad to see you back, get to work!" As he said it a smile crossed his face.

As it was the basic rule in Dachau, he kept to the principle of "the less you know, the better off you are" and did not ask a single question of where I had been or what I had been doing. --- Or did he know?

He told me that he had arranged with Jerzy, the Polish secretary in the next room, to do the most necessary reports, and all other work was waiting for me.

No need to say that there could not have been better news expecting me.

I washed up well in the usual ice-cold water and without wasting time sat down to my small desk and started to catch up with the work. I immediately noticed that office supplies such as pens, pencils, blotters were in much more abundant supply than when I had left. There were even ledger books, which we had never had before.

I questioned Dr. Mueller, but he just waved for me to follow him.

As I entered his small office he motioned toward a new medicine cabinet. Through its glass door a varied supply of medicines were visible, neatly stacked.

Slowly Dr. Mueller started to relate a bizarre story.

"The Nazis agreed to an inspection by the International Red Cross and they are arranging a grand show.

The cabinet is locked and I don't have the key and can not dispense medicine. As a matter of fact I am responsible and had to sign for the inventory. The idea obviously is to convince the Red Cross that the inmates get excellent medical care equivalent to the stipulations of the Geneva Convention. A few sick-rooms have been selected for the "show", I don't know which or how many".

He also related that prisoners in terminal condition from typhus or typhoid fever were being sent to other barracks to improve the "cured" and "survival" rate in the selected sick rooms. The ledger books which I saw on my desk served to contain falsified patient information retroactive to January 1, 1945. The instructions to Dr. Mueller were that the records must show a survival rate of at least 95%. My quick approximate calculation indicated that this would be less than two deaths per week.

As I mentioned earlier, the truth was closer to five deaths per day!!

We were aware of our responsibility in the complicity in this grand fraud to mislead the International Red Cross concerning the conditions in this concentration camp.

We also knew that misleading the Red Cross would lead to the disinformation of the entire civilized world.

However, there was never any question that we had to play our role in this scheme for the sake of our survival.

Records were entered in the ledger to agree with the instructions contained on two sheets of mimeographed instructions.

In conjunction all bed charts were changed to show a variety of ailments from appendicitis to bronchitis to pneumonia (nobody was allowed to have typhus!) The most diabolical invention of the SS was the diagnosis "rest to recuperate".

Dr. Mueller's cubicle was slightly enlarged and the blankets which formed its walls were replaced by wood partitions. Even a small examination table was placed in the center of his office.

White bed sheets and uniform German military blankets were put on all beds.

The floor was washed with a strong-smelling disinfectant.

The superficial impression was that of a standard military hospital room.

THE "POTEMKIN VILLAGE" WAS COMPLETE.

On the morning of the inspection an SS officer in white medical coat showed up and made himself home in Dr. Mueller's office. He curtly explained to Mueller and me that he was the doctor in charge of this room and would respond to all questions of the Red Cross officials. We were always to stay a few steps behind and speak only when he directed a question at us.

During this session of instructions, a technician knocked on the window and reached in a wire with a connector. The SS doctor opened his case and took out a field telephone which he proceeded to hook up.

From the same bag he took out a set of keys and opened the medical supply cabinet.

We were ready for the "show".

The Red Cross inspection took place as scheduled and as all prior actions indicated our sick bay was selected to be visited.

The inspecting team consisted of 6-8 people, always surrounded by at least that many SS officers, some in white coats.

I could hear only fractions of the discussions and the recurring phrases and theme appeared to have been "typical". Apparently the Red Cross people were not too happy about being shown into a sick-bay selected by the SS and wanted to do some random selection. The SS, in turn, kept repeating that this was a typical sick-room and all others were similar.

Upon leaving in an SS military vehicle, they headed toward the "Apellplatz" and the camp gate.

The elaborately planned attempt of misleading the International Red Cross appeared to have been successfully completed.

I have discussed this repeatedly and at length with Dr. Gruen.

Did the Red Cross officials know or suspect the real facts and just went along putting up their own "show" to mislead the Nazis. Was their apparent cooperation only a "front" to keep the Germans off guard?

Was it only an "inspection" to satisfy world opinion without the real aim to discover the truth?

Clearly only an unexpected inspection would have ever had a chance to witness the truth. It was my understanding that this inspection was preceded by months of diplomatic negotiations and, because of that, it never had the least chance of discovering the real facts. Additionally, it was clear that the Germans were in charge and the Red Cross did not have any opportunity to take a single step on their own or to talk to anybody else except the SS.

The International Red Cross saw a great SS stage presentation. All of us were wondering whether they saw through the charade.

Ever since, I very often thought that it would be interesting to discover the resulting official opinion of the International Red Cross.

I certainly hope that at least some members of the International Red Cross (IRC) raised their sights and saw the chimney of the Krematorium belching black smoke. It would have been logical to ask why fires in the Krematorium were always burning if everybody was so well cared for and was so healthy!!!

MINOR SURGERY

One day as I was preparing my note pad and medical forms to follow Dr. Mueller on his morning round, I noticed a slight swelling inside the top knuckle of my right index finger. It was at an uncomfortable position because I could hardly hold the pencil, but I did not think much about it. I labored through the day and slowly and with some pain managed to bring all bed-charts up-to-date after Dr. Mueller's round.

The job took me quite a bit longer than usual, but I wanted to hide this handicap as long as possible and hoped that the swelling would disappear by itself. Disabilities in Dachau were dangerous. They were immediate causes for transfers. In my case it would result in the loss of my assignment as the doctor's secretary and a complete change in my semi-secure position.

Unfortunately, my condition got worse over-night and the swelling became noticeably larger. I felt constant pressure and could move my index finger only with excruciating pain. By morning the entire hand felt hot and stiff.

I realized that there was no way to keep this a secret and as early as I could during the morning I showed the condition to Dr. Mueller. The swelling was the size of a plum by then.

The visibly discolored blood vessels on my lower arm appeared to be disquieting signs for the doctor. He also checked my armpit, but I felt no discomfort.

His decision was, that especially because of the lack of any appropriate medication, immediate surgery was indicated.

He put my right lower arm in a sling and made out a form of requesting surgery.

He said that most surgery of this type was done in Block (barracks) #9 and that he would take me there, since the movement of unaccompanied prisoners within the camp was always dangerous.

He put on his white medical coat (with the proper insignia) and we were on our way.

I do not remember how Dr. Mueller disappeared, but as I entered barracks #9 he was no longer with me.

I found myself in a small room, where a prisoner, apparently working there, took the request for surgery out of my hand .

The man had a Slavic accent and told me in German to move through a door into the next room. The room had nothing in it except small piles of clothing on the floor.

There was nobody there and I felt just like sitting down and falling asleep, hoping that all this was just an unpleasant dream.

My entire arm was aching badly and the constant pressure was often interrupted by sharp piercing pain.

The apparently aimless waiting and the total lack of knowledge of what to expect made my mental state almost unbearable.

After a while, a prisoner-worker came in and told me to get completely undressed and pass through a side door and wait.

I did as I was told while realizing that, while naked, my Jewish identity was obvious.

After putting my clothes in a pile I went through the door that was pointed out to me and found myself in a narrow corridor with about ten naked prisoners standing in line. I joined the queue. I may never have mentioned that I have never seen female prisoners in Dachau, although I was told that there were a very few.

Somebody came and hung around my neck on a string the request for surgery made out by Dr. Mueller.

A door at the front opened and the first naked prisoner was called in.

The silence and the tension in the corridor was overwhelming.

Suddenly, frightening shrieks of pain interrupted the dead silence in the room where we were standing.

It was clear that the room into which the prisoner had just walked was the operating room.

It was also painfully obvious that the operation was being performed without anesthesia, or any local anesthetics of any kind.

The shrieks of pain slowly subsided, possibly because the patient had lost consciousness.

I was frightened. Probably everybody in the waiting line was.

However, there was no way back, no way out, no alternatives.

During the hours that followed similar sounds of pain were repeatedly heard after a new patient went into the operating room.

I wished to faint to be released from this mental cruelty and suffering, but I clearly remember that exactly the opposite occurred. My senses were keen, I was aware of every detail. I even seemed to hear the silence.

Finally it was my turn. I went into the operating room. A doctor and a helper were present. The doctor wore a full-length white coat, the helper a short white jacket, both over camp uniforms.

The doctor gave a quick glance to the "request for surgery" now hanging from my neck and abruptly squeezed the bluish carbuncle on my hand. I cried out in pain.

The doctor signaled to the helper, who came and put a piece of wood in front of my mouth and said: "bite", I did.

I guess this was instead of anesthetics.

They tied my lower arm to the surface of a small operating table with leather bands.

The doctor quickly made an incision of about two inches long into the discolored and greatly swollen carbuncle.

I bit down as hard as I could on the wood in my mouth and the only sound that escaped was a muffled cry of agony.

The doctor scraped some and squeezed hard on the boil, expelling a lot of ugly, bloody pus.

All this time I was looking on, essentially frozen stiff. Only when I saw him reach for needle and thread did I realize that it might be better to turn away. I sensed the leather bands being released and felt that the doctor had started bandaging. I turned my head back toward him.

He looked at me and said: "Finished, all is well, Dr. Mueller can remove the drain and the stitches in a few days." Without giving me an Aspirin to reduce the pain, he turned away to wash his hands.

My nerves just started to catch up with my mind. With trembling legs and shaking all over I was pushed through another door and ended up in the room with the small piles of clothes.

I had a splitting headache and felt like just sitting or lying down and not doing anything, (hopefully, just sleeping), but my desire to get out of here was stronger. Using my left hand I got dressed.

I was in no shape to think logically and it never occurred to me that I should not be moving alone between barracks. I opened the door and slowly walked back to my sick bay in barracks #15. Only when I entered the room did someone tell me that I still had my chart hanging around my neck. I removed it. A small note was attached for the attention of Dr. Mueller to remove the drain and the stitches after a few days.

Thanks to God's help, to youth, and probably to the expert (but not kind) medical care, rendered by a fellow Jewish prisoner (as I found out later), my hand improved rapidly. However, after 50 years a scar is still evident.

CRIME AND PUNISHMENT?

A brief and sad episode occurred shortly after my surgery. One morning a Kapo deposited a small blond, almost white, curly haired, youngster of about 12-14 years old in our room. He was feverish but conscious and completely coherent. He said his name was Erich Berger. He was German and certainly looked more Aryan than Hitler.

This is his own story as I remember it:

His father had been a soldier and had died on the Russian front. His mother had died recently in a burning ruin during an air raid on Munich.

He was hungry and had stolen a loaf of bread at a market. He was apprehended, unluckily for him, not by local police, but by a group of loitering and drunk SS soldiers who delivered their own justice by beating him black and blue all over the face, legs and back.

The soldiers were apparently stationed in Dachau and brought the kid with them. They must have gotten concerned when they slept off the alcohol and turned him over to their commanding officer, who after some phone calls decreed that the child be turned in at the concentration camp.

After having been processed as an "undesirable juvenile" he was brought to our sick-bay because he was suspected of coming down with typhus.

Since the only thing we could offer him was rest, aspirin and charcoal tablets, the illness, whatever it was, took its course and Erich Berger died in about a week.

It goes without saying that the punishment did not fit the crime of a hungry youngster who stole a loaf of bread.

Erich Berger was a sad casualty of the extremes of war in general, and a typical example of the inhuman Nazi mentality, where life was worth nothing, even if it was German.

ESCAPE!!!
SAVING A GOOD LIFE

Most of the accounts described occurred during my imprisonment in the Dachau concentration camp, but to complete the picture I plan to relate events which happened long after the liberation.

It goes without saying that there was no such thing as certainty in Dachau unless one gave up all hope and was certain to perish.

However, having an assignment in one of the hospital barracks was as far removed from an unexpected catastrophe as could be within the electric fence of the concentration camp. My job as a doctor's secretary was such a job.

There were immediate dangers, mainly represented by prisoners who were (or were suspected to be) Nazi informers. One such person was the Dutch barber, Jan. It is entirely possible that all of us assumed him to be an informer because of circumstance.

He was authorized of free movement within the camp and was often seen to enter into and spend time in the SS barracks. His "home base" was in our sick-bay and we often questioned him about his activities. He related that he had been in the camp for several years, having been arrested in his home town of Rhenen in Holland for anti-Nazi activities.

In the camp he used his professional skill as a barber to provide services to a few German guards and slowly became so popular with the Germans that he carried an appointment book.

One morning he was next to me in the washroom and after looking at my naked body, asked: "Do they know that you are a Jew?" He did not seem to wait for an answer, but his remark suddenly created the jitters in me. I rubbed myself off rapidly with ice cold water and got dressed in record time.

This might be an opportune time to relate that cleanliness often meant the difference between life and death in Dachau because washing tended to destroy (or keep away) typhus-carrying lice on your body.

For me the rub-down with ice cold water in the middle of winter in an (of course) unheated wash room was an exercise in will-power. It was, however, evident by observation that the incidence of typhus was much higher in those prisoners who did not wash their entire bodies daily and thoroughly with cold water. No need to say that there was no warm water and we had to be happy to have a wash room at all.

The memories of these cold water rub-downs became a phobia with me and ever since, taking a hot bath every night has become a psychological compulsion and not a hygienic exercise.

One morning Jan the barber came to my desk and said that he would be back from his barbering jobs during the middle of the afternoon and wanted to talk to me.

His attitude appeared to be neutral, even friendly, but I could not help remembering his observation in the wash room.

I was nervous and on-edge all day and had trouble paying attention to Dr. Mueller's dictation, to the point that I often had to ask him to repeat his remarks. He obviously noticed my lack of concentration and looked at me with a kind of surprised expression several times.

The barber was sitting at my desk when I returned from the rounds with Dr. Mueller.

"I want you to help four of my friends escape" he blurted out.

I had two instant impressions, both frightening. The first was him using the word "want", which indicated that I was under his control and had no option of saying "no".

The second was the subject itself.

How could I help anybody escape??

Why had he chosen me for this task? What were my qualifications?

Did he consider me dispensable and was this a job of no return?

Was he part of some type of organization with connections to the Nazis?

I swallowed hard and considered my options, if any.

I could just say "no" and try to force a response out of him. I could then first and foremost find out more about the proposal and could make up my mind whether the risk was within reason.

The second approach was to agree without any questions or objections in hope of creating good will.

I said fairly quickly that whatever my role might be in an escape plan I did not see what my qualifications were.

"You satisfy two important qualifications. You speak German and your face looks fairly similar to someone's.

He pulled his chair closer to my desk and began his story. He had found out that a small work detail of about twenty prisoners went every night to clean up at the power station which heated the entire SS complex.

Tonight the work detail would be accompanied by one SS guard, who was not from the usual command and did not know anybody by sight. The power station was within the SS compound (although well outside the concentration camp). Military security would be less than usual today.

The plan was to give me the identification papers of a German trustee prisoner to act as the leader of the work detail and as a contact with the SS guard.

The overall scheme of the escape plan was very simple. It was known that the work detail of twenty prisoners was to be staged in front of the reception building. I was to show up as a trustee prisoner in charge. I would be accompanied by the four "friends" of Jan, the barber, who planned to escape. I was to lead the complete group of 24 into the reception building where I would report that the powerhouse work detail was ready for duty.

I had two instant questions. Where would the trustee be who was really supposed to be in charge?

The barber's answer was simple, rapid and to the point. "Very drunk" -- he smiled.

My second question was what would happen if the SS guard counted off the group and found that there were 24 people and not twenty as reported.

Jan was ready with an answer.

"The start of an escape is always only a plan which may or may not succeed. If there is a head count by the SS it will take place in the reception building within the gates of the concentration camp. At that point no escape or crime will have been committed as yet. Your job will be to select my friends "randomly" and have them march back to the holding area in the building, where I will have made preparations in case the plan fails".

He also assured me that the SS man was one of his shaving clients and was not likely to count the men.

The first stage of the escape plan was so simple that it appeared to me it had a chance of succeeding.

However, in the main, my agreement was based on the fact that I was in his hands because he knew that I was masquerading as a German while being a Jew.

Not agreeing to participate in his plan could have exposed me to serious danger.

My next question was that since I would be away from about 6 p.m. to until early next morning, how I would explain this to Dr. Mueller?

To my surprise the barber's answer was:" Leave it to me, the doctor and I understand each other!"

This was the first time that I considered that Dr. Mueller was holding out on me. It also became conceivable that there might be more to this benevolent-appearing man than met the eye. It was also evident that knowing more was likely to be of no benefit to me.

I agreed. Jan told me that I would find the trustee identification and the names of the twenty prisoners in the drawer of my desk before 5 p.m. At the same time he gave me the names of his four "friends". He warned me not to put the trustee identification on the outside of my jacket before I was out of the sick-room.

"You will see the group of the twenty prisoners in front of the right hand door of the reception building. Be there at 6 p.m. As you cross the Appelplatz my four friends will join you. Take command!! Behave like a Kapo. Speak only German. Set the prisoners up in military order."

"Report to the SS desk sergeant or the bookkeeper trustee that the power-house cleaning detail is ready."

I was tense, nervous and not a little frightened. I even thought of leaving behind a note of explanation for Dr. Mueller, but my new-found doubts in him prevented me from doing so. I started to doubt that I should share everything with Dr. Mueller. It was also clear that putting anything in writing could be plain suicide.

With the necessary identification papers in my pockets I moved out of the sick-bay shortly before 6 p.m..

All went according to the script as defined by Jan, the barber. I felt like an actor playing a role. For a few seconds I even forgot to be afraid.

Upon reporting in, the chief trustee barked "wait outside".

I was happy to get out of his sight and moved out.

We were shortly joined by an SS soldier.

I shouted "ACHTUNG" and had the group stand to attention.

I reported in my best, well-rehearsed German that the power house detail, was ready.

"Roll call" commanded the SS man.

This was not expected and I realized that I might have made a major mistake by not using the list given to me by the barber for a trial roll-call before reporting in with the work detail.

However, this was water under the bridge and I whipped out my list from my pocket and started to call out names. Upon the "Yes, here" response to the first name a gigantic stone fell from my chest.

All twenty names responded and I turned to the SS and reported that all were present and accounted for. Luckily it did not occur to him to compare the number of names with the actual head count (which would have been four too many) and ordered us to start toward the camp gate (ARBEIT MACHT FREI).

The central power house with its tall round brick chimney was visible even in the darkness from the camp gate and the direction and route were evident. Additionally, I understood that several prisoners had been in this detail before and knew all about the jobs to be performed. I decided that my best approach was to let them go through their routines.

We passed several SS military buildings. One of them was a 4-5 story large L-shaped brick structure.

After crossing a bridge over a small creek we were just about under the tall red brick chimney of the power house.

I did not know what the formalities were to gain entrance, but luckily the SS soldier took the initiative and moved ahead. After he had opened a door we followed and I let those prisoners familiar with the job run the show.

We were in a large multi-storied structure.

There were three huge stationary steam power plants next to each other.

I was amazed to see that they were BABCOCK-WILCOX water tube steam boilers, one of the best in the world and probably manufactured in Brooklyn, New York.

As an inmate of Dachau concentration camp and as a Jew I tended to see the war as between good and evil. Either black or white!! No shades of gray.

I just could not understand that commercial contact and cooperation existed between the two sides. After all, these boilers, probably worth millions of dollars, were not sold to a German city or to German civilians, but directly to the German SS, known to be the prime power base and executioners of Hitler's evil goals.

But at this moment this was only philosophy.

I had to concentrate on my mission, the assistance in the escape of four prisoners.

I noticed that the work ticket had to be signed by the chief engineer (or assistant) of the power plant. Having the ticket in my hand I walked up one of the open stair cases where I assumed the offices were. The stairs ended at a height of about ten feet. Here the right and left hand stair cases were connected by a narrow over-view terrace at about half the height of the giant power-plants Walking around with the supposedly only aim of obtaining the necessary signature, I was trying to find a rear, hopefully unguarded, entrance to the offices.

I was lucky because I noticed two exterior fire ladders from the top of the building and passing in front of the windows at the level of the terrace on which I was standing.

Much of the view to these windows was blocked by the giant boilers. Our SS guard appeared to have been concentrating on his copy of the official Nazi paper, the Voelkischer Beobachter. Opening the windows and reaching to the fire escape appeared to be possible.

While on the terrace level I explored some corridors. Behind a lighted half glass door I saw an elderly man sitting behind a desk. Probably the night-duty engineer. I knocked and entered. He saw the ticket in my hand and knew what I had came for. He reached out and signed the paper.

I descended to the main floor where one group was wet-mopping the tile and cement floor and the other cleaning work benches and tools with oiled rags.

I approached one of the Dutchmen called Nathan and waved to him to follow me. I told him that the progress of the work indicated that we should be finished in about an hour and that our work papers were already signed. I informed him about the fire escapes and it became clear to me that he knew about them much sooner than I did and it was part of their plan.

It did not surprise me that like all Dutchmen he understood German completely well, but was amazed that he also spoke it well, although with a strange accent. Using the old German miners' greeting, "Glueck auf", I slowly walked away.

The four, pails and mops in hand, I moved up the stairs toward the fire escapes.

At this very second a frightening thought crossed my mind, something that I had never considered before!

What if all did <u>not</u> go well with the escape plan and all or some got caught, wounded or killed.

How would I explain that I still had all 20 of my work team??!!

There was no doubt in my mind that before starting back to the camp the SS would order a head-count. Also I had to expect a second head-count by the guards at the camp gate.

I was aware that Jan the barber had considered this possibility. If he had thought of it and not mentioned it to me, there was obviously no answer and the consequence would be the loss of my life. I would likely be accused of organizing the entire escape attempt, or at least of being of material assistance to it.

And what about the trustee identification which really was not mine? It was only good until somebody closely compared me with the description on the identification.

It was a clever escape plan, surely planned in every detail.

However, it was also evident that Jan's master plan called for a "disposable" figure and I was IT.

Jan, the barber, surely was not my friend and part of his consideration must have been that one Jew more or less made no difference.

I decided to make a run for it via the fire-escape ladder if the escape was discovered.

There was no noise, no shouting and most importantly no shooting. With every passing moment it became more likely that the escape would be successful.

It was close to 4 a.m., the end of the shift. I called the team together and ordered them to collect and store their cleaning equipment. At the same time I selected two prisoners to follow me because I knew that there must be four buckets and mops somewhere near the windows leading to the fire escapes. I underestimated the four escapees. After some search we found the buckets and the mops, as well as a container of cleaning powder, in a small storage room behind the barrels of oil and cans of grease stored for the maintenance of the boilers. We collected the equipment and without anybody saying a single word, descended the steps and added the cleaning utensils to the others located in a wash-room reserved for this purpose.

"Roll call!" shouted the SS guard.

I took over instantly and set up the work group in five rows of four each. I walked along the small work detail and called out the numbers in a loud voice: 4--8--12--16--20.

I wanted to give the guard a good show and also called out the 20 names. 20 "Jawohls" followed.

For a moment I did not know what the next step was. Luckily the guard very obviously held out his hand and I realized that I was supposed to gave him the list.

As I approached him and, standing to attention, stretched out my arm and handed him the list, he commanded: "Return to camp!"

It was about 4 a. m. and I had to order my work detail to move to the side since the prisoner detail which operated and maintained the boilers was about to come through the main entrance.

At about 5 a. m. our SS guard signaled and the camp gate (ARBEIT MACHT FREI) opened.

He reported to the SS sergeant of the guard that the power house cleaning detail of 20 men had returned.

The sergeant did a quick head count, appeared to make an entry into a book and waved us through.

I marched the men to the building where I had picked them up and instantly realized that I did not know what my next move should be.

I had no idea of the formalities, rules and regulations that applied to a trustee prisoner (a role which I was now playing), upon returning a work detail. Any wrong, unusual or uncalled-for move could bring instant adverse reaction by the SS and I had to consider that my "trustee identification" was good only until somebody looked at it closely. It was not even the picture which was a dead give-away. There was a definite resemblance between its owner and me. Additionally, the pass was so worn that the picture could fit practically anyone. The main problem was running into someone, SS or Kapo who knew the owner of the pass personally.

I decided to wait. In a short while another work detail was brought in by two trustee prisoners. They just waved to the bookkeeper-administrator trustee sitting at a desk, turned around and walked out.

Blending into the routine seemed the best approach and I made a circle around the room, appearing to read the announcements tagged on the wall, walked by the desk, waved and turned toward the door.

"What happened to Rudi?" The question came from the administrator at the desk and was obviously directed at me since there was nobody in the vicinity.

My heart skipped a beat! Disaster! The trustee identification in my pocket was Rudi's!!

"He is sick", I said finally and it was I who felt very sick.

Probably drunk, like most of the time, said the trustee at the desk. "They will catch up with him sooner or later unless he stops it" he said smiling.

"Give my regards to Jan, and remind him that he skipped my shave yesterday."

I continued to realize that an escape from Dachau was a complex operation organized in probably endless numbers of details and I was only a very small part of the overall execution. There appeared to be many "cells", none of which knew about the other.

In my opinion the top man was Jan the barber. He was probably the only person who was aware of all details that made up the complete picture.

Was the easy-going SS man also part of the scheme?

How come there were no guards at the rear of the power house which was less than 300 feet from the perimeter of the SS camp?

These were just some of the obvious questions about this escape and even if I could find the answers, I thought it was safer not to know.

With these thoughts in mind I walked out the door of the reception area and headed for barracks #15, sick bay #2.

I had left the previous evening just about twelve hours ago and shortly before 7 a. m. I was back at my desk.

I was exhausted. Not so much my body as my mind. I decided that I had time to wash and rest on my bed for a few minutes before starting my day with Dr. Mueller.

One of my instant decisions was to make sure that my attitude toward Dr. Mueller should not change in any way.

At the same moment the door of the sick-room opened and Jan the barber came in and without any delay headed to me.

Compared with the former mental picture of this man I saw a different person approaching me.

"Thank you for your help, all is well, all four are out and safe for the time being."

"I am sorry that I had to create doubt and possibly fear in you to gain your cooperation, but escapes from camps are complex and often ruthless exercises. The fact that I found out that you were Jewish gave me the handle that I needed to enlist you in the plan. However, just to prove a point, one of the escaped prisoners was Nathan the baker, my Jewish neighbor. His entire family are old friends of ours in Holland."

I felt sick. Somehow the more he spoke, the more he tried to justify his actions, the less I believed him. It all seemed to be a professionally rehearsed play. The details appeared to fit together much too conveniently. In spite of the points he made, it was clear that the entire operation would not have been possible without the knowledge and cooperation of the SS.

He then asked me for the trustee identification which he had given me the night before. I handed it to him. He picked up the scissors from my desk and cut it up into several pieces which he put into his pocket.

Upon my questioning look he simply stated: "He will not need it any more".

With the above short statement he closed the subject and left all else to my imagination.

Jan got up and headed for the wash-room, probably to dispose of the small slivers of paper, formerly including the photograph of someone by the name of Rudi.

After this conversation, no direct or indirect reference was ever made to this event.

A few hours after liberation I saw Jan talking to a group of prisoners. I tried to approach him, but as soon as he noticed me he quickly moved away and disappeared in the crowd. I never saw him again.

About a year after the liberation of the concentration camp, I was told that a military convoy would be heading for Amsterdam from the Dachau military post. I also found out that they were routed through, or near Rhenen, the home town of Jan the barber and according to him also of Nathan and his family.

It took several interviews and some convincing of friends and friends of friends until I succeeded in arranging to become part of the convoy as an interpreter.

The captain in command agreed to drop me off in Rhenen on the way to Amsterdam and pick me up a couple of days later on their way back.

In Rhenen we stopped in front of a building flying the Dutch national flag. It turned out to be a combination of a town hall, school and the offices of several refugee organizations trying to find quarters for citizens returning home after having been displaced by the war. They also served as a clearing house to bring together local families separated for whatever reason during the war.

Thanks to my US uniform (although without any insignia) nobody asked me who I was and I had no trouble setting up my blankets and back-pack in the corner of a room which appeared to have been a library at one time.

General confusion raged because there were so many organizations in the building that nobody appeared to know who was who and nobody was in charge.

For sentimental reasons my priority was to find Nathan and for this objective I tried to locate a bakery and ask questions.

I discovered that this was easier said than done. I attempted to speak English, but although I encountered a lot of sympathy I found that hardly anybody had sufficient working knowledge of the language.

I then tried to speak German, but understandably that turned out to be (and very logically so) impractical.

After their country had been occupied, practically destroyed, ransacked, and some of their daughters and wives raped by the Germans, I could hardly expect them to make cheerful contact with someone who spoke German to them.

Walking along, I found a bakery and walked in with a carefully prepared plan.

I repeated the word American for a few times and after they responded "no English" I started to speak a mixture of poor English and German. I knew that German and Dutch were similar and was sure that they understood at least part of what I was saying. I also put a couple of packs of American cigarettes on the counter and indicated by a few words and some sign-language that they were for them.

I then tried to explain to them that I was looking for a friend, a baker, by the name of Nathan. I saw a sign of relief and recognition on their faces and without any further theatrics I told them that I had been in Dachau concentration camp with Nathan and had helped him escape.

Subsequently I briefly described my identity and as we went on the conversation became friendlier and got more and more German, since it was obvious that at least the two younger men, Pieter and Harmen understood it perfectly.

Yes, they knew Nathan. His family had never returned from "deportation", but Nathan and a younger brother were in Rhenen.

Although they seemed to trust me they were concerned about Nathan's safety. They asked me to prove to them that I knew him.

The bakery was in a small side street only two or three houses away from a main street with some pedestrian traffic.

A quick and practical idea helped me. I begged them to arrange for Nathan to walk on the main street and while I stood at their shop door I would point him out.

Harmen, one of the youngsters, volunteered to get Nathan and left at once.

They said if Nathan was home and was available he could be around in less than half an hour.

I had a few candy bars in my pockets and we had a little party while we waited.

Harmen came back in a few minutes and told me to start observing the street. His shining face clearly revealed that he had spoken to Nathan and Nathan had confirmed my story.

It took somewhat longer than we expected and I started to believe that I had missed him, when he showed up crossing the street.

I shouted his name as loud as I could and he instantly started to run toward me.

It was an emotional meeting and the entire family that helped us find each other was crying.

It took Nathan a long time to fill me in about the happenings after the escape from the power house in Dachau. He told me that all of them got as far as the Amper river behind the SS camp, where they found a small row boat hidden in the reeds. They silently got into the boat and waited until the SS patrol on the opposite side moved beyond hearing range.

They slowly pushed the boat through the reeds and using a seat found in the boat rowed and pushed the boat across the small river.

The description of their long journey through Germany, full of hair-raising experiences, cannot be part of this narrative.

It is evident, however, that during the early months of 1945 there were at least some Germans who saw that it was only a question of a few months until the total collapse and end of the "1000 year" Third Reich. Many Germans offered help or at least neutrality to the four refugees.

The greatest news of the day was when Nathan related that Jan the barber had been arrested by the Dutch police shortly after his arrival in Rhenen on suspicion of widespread and traitorous cooperation with the Nazis.

Something did not fit. Why had Jan helped Nathan? I asked him as soon as I thought of it. It was clear that the escape was for the benefit of people of attitudes similar to those of Jan.

"I overheard the plan and confronted them. They included me to buy my silence. Jan knew me, or knew of me, because my father was a religious man and a leading member of the Jewish community" I suddenly understood Nathan's nearly perfect German with the unique accent. It was Yiddish!!

I remembered my doubts and suspicions about Jan and was sure that what I had assumed and witnessed was only the tip of the iceberg of this Nazi collaborator.

Nathan's parents and a sister had disappeared during the war, probably taken by the Nazis and he had had no news about them, but still hoped. His younger brother survived the war in Rhenen with the help of Dutch neighbors.

I have never heard of Nathan since and, although we only met twice in our lives, once in the Dachau power house and once that afternoon in Rhenen, in a Dutch bakery, I will always remember him because I think that GOD gave me the opportunity to save a good life.

THE LIBERATION

It was during early March 1945 that news of Allied victories started to permeate the camp. Prisoners whose jobs allowed some movement between barracks began to become less frightened and more talkative. I found out from the Polish plumber that the former Polish officers had a radio and had heard that the Americans had crossed the Rhine.

It required little knowledge of geography and military strategy to know that if the Germans could not defend their only natural defense line, the Rhine, they were on the verge of total defeat.

However, the paramount question in our minds remained whether the SS would eliminate all inmates of the concentration camp as a last act of senseless cruelty.

Some of us even wondered whether they might burn or blow up the entire camp so as not to leave any trace of this hell hole.

News came from prisoners working in the SS military camp that all railroad sidings were full of regular passenger coaches. This indicated that they were likely to be intended for the evacuation of SS families and personnel.

The Germans based most of the camp order and discipline on trustee prisoners.

In order to prove their trustworthiness to the Germans, some of them made it a point to exceed the SS in cruelty and inhuman behavior toward the prisoners. It is obvious that some of them considered this nothing more than their "ticket" to survival, but it is more than questionable that this justified their actions.

This was the first stage at which the camp organization broke down. Most of the Kapos moved to barracks where they were not known, or by some other means faded into anonymity. In spite of this I heard that some of them were hanged by former prisoners after the liberation.

Without the presence of the Kapos some prisoners started to move around on their own in the camp.

Day after day the war news, now circulating almost freely, indicated significant Allied advances.

The mood of the prisoners improved, especially when we noticed that the guard towers were seldom manned by the SS.

I heard that somebody even tried the electrified fence which surrounded the camp and found that it was no longer charged.

One morning, when I was getting ready for the morning "round" with Dr. Mueller, a young man in white coat over prisoner garb came up to my desk and introduced himself as Dr. Francois. I don't think I ever found out whether this was his first or last name. Responding to my puzzled face he said:" Dr. Mueller is no longer here".

To make sure that there was no opportunity for a question, he added that we would start the rounds in about an hour and that he would call me.

Absolutely nothing could have shocked me more than the news about Dr. Mueller.

I considered him and his former assistant Paul as the people who were primarily responsible for my still being alive.

What happened to the doctor?

Had he been arrested? Was there an informer in the room who had caused his down-fall because he told me too much about the background and circumstances of the Red Cross inspection?

Probably not, because then I would have been arrested as well.

Had he been transferred?

Most unlikely, because he would have known it ahead of time and even if he had not told me explicitly, he would have hinted at the possibility.

Had he been arrested because he was too humane, or because of his frequent remarks about the lack of proper medical care?

Not probable, that would have happened much earlier.

Had he decided to escape?

Possibly.

Was his humanity an assumed facade? Was he in effect a German informer who had decided that the game was up and it was time to disappear?

I just did not want to believe this last possibility, but I realized that my opinion was entirely subjective.

I was distressed and totally confused. The only thing I was sure about was that I should never ask anybody and never make any related remark.

My knowledge about Dr. Francois was only enlarged by his remark that he was Belgian.

For the past few days the sky had been full of planes and the sound of constant bombing and anti-aircraft fire. The night sky in the direction of Munich was lit up by fires almost like daylight.

One day, standing in front of the barracks door, I saw an Allied plane hit by German anti-aircraft fire. The plane trailed heavy smoke for a while and then exploded in the air.

I knew that the war had not been fought to save Jews, but in the absence of a cap, I put my hand on my head and prayed for the ever-lasting peace of those who died for us in that plane.

The watch towers were no longer occupied, but there was still some occasional SS truck traffic through the main gate.

Dr. Francois and I were sitting on the steps of our sick room. In a short while my original mentor Paul joined us. It was a beautiful spring afternoon on April 28, 1945. Between the occasional sound of a truck passing through the camp gate there was total silence.

Suddenly the sounds of far-away explosions broke the silence. We were subconsciously so accustomed to the sounds of air raids (the concentration camp itself was never bombed) that we kept talking about the most common subject of those last days in the concentration camp. Would the SS flee, put up resistance, or just blow us all up?

Then something in the nature of the sounds made us listen. This was not a distant air raid, these were salvos of artillery interspersed with machine- gun fire.

The front was within earshot!!

Our chances of survival suddenly looked infinitely better.

Our liberators were within a stone's throw.

I wiped my tears off my face and looked at Paul and Dr. Francois. They were also crying.

As darkness fell, artillery fire lit up the horizon and was added to the sounds.

Nobody went to sleep that night in sick bay #2 Block #15. The room was completely quiet. We all felt that history was being made around us. Tears of joy were shining on many silent faces.

There were hardly any shots heard, the SS appeared to have fled. Many of them must have obtained civilian clothes. In the ensuing days we found their uniforms in the guard towers and in their barracks.

Next day, on April 29, 1945, odd-looking small vehicles (as we found out later they were called jeeps) full of US soldiers of the 42 US Rainbow Division surrounded the camp.

We were liberated.

I was fortunate to meet fifty years later in 1995 some members of the 42nd Division, who were actually in Dachau on the day of our liberation in 1945. The occasion was the memorial celebration arranged by the Bavarian Government in Munich.

DANGER
HIGH VOLTAGE

I believe that the population of Dachau concentration camp at the time of the liberation was about 40,000.

The US troops were well prepared for the liberation of the concentration camp. The wide-spread typhus epidemic appeared to have been known to them and was confirmed by the first American contacts, most of whom were medical specialists.

As I mentioned before, the concentration camp was surrounded on two sides by a large SS military installation. This entire facility now became an American Military Post and part of this area was used as a general medical rehabilitation center for the former prisoners.

The procedure started with disinfecting, showers, baths and other treatments to get rid of lice and other infection carriers. Fresh clothing was issued to all. Individual medical examinations and treatment were provided. A hospital was also maintained for those former concentration camp inmates who needed intensive medical care.

The former SS barracks were thoroughly disinfected and became our first quarters.

The average weight of a prisoner in Dachau at the time of the liberation was less than 100 pounds. All prisoners that I had ever seen were male. It is said that there was an insignificant number of female inmates, but I never saw any.

For the first hours or days after liberation the starved former prisoners who had dreamed about food for months and years associated the Americans first with food and only after that with freedom.

The Americans knew, however, that a weakened and starved body must be built up gradually and rationed the food to avoid gastric or abdominal diseases.

I have described my relationship and contacts with Laszlo Bekeffy the former Hungarian stage personality and well known anti-Nazi political satirist. He was alive and reasonably well at the time of liberation (still in sick-bay #2 in Block #15)

As usual, he played the hypochondriac and was taken to the American hospital.

At any rate, I did not have to make the "most confidential" phone call to London .

I must admit that I had not quite believed Bekeffy's spy story when he had first told it to me some months previously.

Things were beginning to change now. About ten days after liberation a British ambulance arrived in Dachau. In the US Zone of Occupation, especially at the Dachau Military Post, this was most unusual.

The ambulance came specifically to get Mr. Bekeffy.

I guess I had been wrong to doubt him and, considering the individual attention that he got from the British, I started to believe that he was indeed part of the British Secret Service in Hungary.

It was about that time that posters appeared in English and several other languages stating that the US troops would organize a Post Utilities section and would hire former inmates with a knowledge of construction, metal-working machinery, electrical work, plumbing and other technical skills. Knowledge of English was required for some positions.

After graduating from high school in Hungary, I applied for admission to the Technical University, but this was only a formality, since it was self evident that as a Jew I would not be admitted.

As a technically inclined youth, I completed an apprenticeship as a precision mechanic and as a consequence I was thoroughly familiar with all types of metal-working machinery. As a further qualification toward the jobs posted by the Americans, I spoke English reasonably well as a result of four years of high school English and extensive private studies.

The interview was conducted in English by a US major of the Corps of Engineers. After a few minutes of stuttering, to my own amazement I started to overcome my nerves and had no trouble in either understanding him or expressing myself in reasonably fluent English. My technical background and knowledge of English, German and Hungarian turned out to be a winning combination and I was hired as the major's administrative assistant.

The original scope of my job was the administration of labor assignments and liaison between the US command and the indigenous labor, mainly to overcome the language barrier. However, it developed into something much more meaningful in a brief period. It seems that technically qualified US military personnel were very hard to get and those who were selected by the major were transferred to other duties within the military, or were discharged.

To avoid having to deal with this constant turn-over of military personnel, the major gave me additional authorities and duties.

In a reasonably short time I was responsible for all organizational matters, hiring, personnel appointments, housing assignments, work schedules, budgeting, equipment and all reporting to the military command. The major gave guidelines and within those I had a wide latitude to operate. Not lastly, I was paid in military dollars (script) at a time when the German Reichsmark was losing its value by the day.

It was an amazing job for a young man of 21. It was also the first time in my life that being Jewish did not disqualify me, or represent a hurdle.

One of the first jobs of the Post Utilities Department was to prepare the former concentration camp as housing for the German SS prisoners of war taken by the US troops. This work also included building about thirty large new barracks. When the Post Utilities workers got through with the renovation, the SS prisoners of war moved into a camp which was in excellent sanitary condition, was not crowded and offered reasonably comfortable quarters for all.

I allowed myself one liberty, which was countermanded by the US command as soon as they found out about it. I assigned several electricians to check out and if necessary repair the high-voltage electric fence around the camp. I also arranged for wooden signs every 30 feet along the inside perimeter of the fence.

DANGER
HIGH VOLTAGE

When all was complete I went to the main gate (ARBEIT MACHT FREI) and personally turned on the power.

It may have been a theatrical action on my part and on order of my US superiors it had to be undone immediately.

However, even today I feel that it was a justified symbolic gesture.

WAR CRIMES TRIALS

Everybody knew of and many followed with interest the Nuremberg War Crimes Trials of 1946.

Very few were aware that about the same time lesser rank, but possibly not less guilty war criminals were being tried by US Military Tribunals in Dachau. The various tribunals had their sessions in different buildings.

The trials in Dachau were low key procedures and the audience at times was smaller than the size of the tribunal.

An exception was the ILSE KOCH ("THE BITCH OF BUCHENWALD") trial.

(See footnote # 3)

At most routine trials, occasionally, the only spectator was the reporter from the STARS AND STRIPES newspaper. It was amazing how well informed he was about all the trials going on in Dachau.

I was a daily cover-to-cover reader of THE STARS & STRIPES not only to be up-to-date with the news, but also because it was my best source for learning English, especially spelling.

As an employee of the Dachau US Military Post I had little involvement with the trials and knew very little about the proceedings. My only active interest was the supervision of some interior modifications of the buildings where the trials took place.

Footnote # 3

ILSE KOCH was the wife of the camp commander of Buchenwald and was tried for crimes against humanity.

See APPENDIX

One afternoon this was changed by a phone call of the Office of the Judge Advocate. The colonel had a simple statement and a couple of questions:

"Your personal files indicate that you speak English, German and Hungarian. Do you speak Hungarian fluently?" My response was that Hungarian was my mother-tongue. "Do you speak English fluently?" I answered that I had a pretty good vocabulary and spoke English exactly as they heard me now, including the Hungarian accent. I also added that I was not particularly familiar with specialized legal terms in English.

My responses were apparently satisfactory and they asked me whether I could be at the Judge Advocate's office within one half hour. In a few minutes I was on my way.

The Assistant J. A., a Lt. Colonel, introduced me to two captains. One of them started to explain to me the reason for my presence. The other was the US Prosecutor in this trial.

The trial of a small group of SS men was to start the coming Monday. One of the SS men, defended by a German attorney assigned by the Court, had unexpectedly decided the day before that he wished to be questioned and to make his statements to the Court in Hungarian, because he spoke and understood it better than German. The prosecution first assumed that it was only a ploy to gain time, but upon review it turned out that he was an ethnic German from Hungary and his request for a Hungarian Court translator was approved.

The personnel operating the simultaneous-instant translation system of the Court were English-German, German-English only.

Now, in order not to have to reschedule a whole string of trials, they needed somebody to translate between English and Hungarian. Luckily all German defense attorneys on this case were certified in English.

They almost agreed that I was the quick-fix for the problem, but nobody could come up with a valid procedure to test my knowledge of Hungarian!

They were somewhat befuddled for a few minutes, but the colonel offered a cut-through solution for the Gordian knot.

"Mr. Wassermann learned English and all of us are totally satisfied with his knowledge of it. Clearly, Hungarian being his mother-tongue, he speaks it better than English. I think it is completely fair to both the defense and the prosecution to certify him."

"We will make-out the certification now and I will speak to the presiding officer of the Court before Monday and bring him up-to-date."

I was in the lobby of the court almost an hour before the trial was to start, my stomach full of butterflies.

It went through my mind that during my service in Hungarian forced labor and my stay in Dachau, I had very often willingly taken life-threatening risks without being nervous about what the consequences might be. Now, before being an essentially uninvolved and totally unthreatened participant in a trial I was tense and unstrung.

I guess I had re-entered civilization!!

The court came to order and I was given my certification. One of the first steps of the procedure was to swear me in. Obviously I do not remember the exact text, although I carried a copy with me for many years. It included that I would translate everything to the best of my ability and no personal feeling or opinion that I might have about what I had to translate would in any way interfere with the "truest possible" translation of the words.

All SS men, I think there were six or so, were accused of atrocities including killings during a marching transport of mostly but not exclusively Jewish concentration camp inmates. They were identified after the liberation by survivors of the march.

The defense, as usual, was based on the routine German argument of almost all war criminals. They were following orders.

In this case, the particular order was to shoot anybody who after a single warning could not or would not get up and keep up the pace of the march.

It seems that some of these cruel bastards wanted to do better than the orders and shot people who stopped and bent down to adjust their foot-wear, people who moved to the sides of the marching column to catch more wind or fresh air, people who stopped to urinate, or those who just by happenstance at a particular moment were walking in the last rows of the column. It also came out during the trial that three prisoners were shot because two of them had reached under the arms of a third who otherwise could not have kept up.

My role was to translate, and not to judge the merits of the arguments, when "my" man was being questioned or making statements, was a tough job. I realized that it was entirely different to speak a language, even to master a language, than to act as a court translator, where every word had to be contemplated to make sure that it was the best possible translation of the defendant's statement. I stressed the word translation because I got stuck with it more than once.

At one point, the US Attorney wanted to clarify a point and appeared to ask the same question in several different ways. "My" defendant essentially repeated his same answer in Hungarian, but the second time, used different words. I tried to differentiate between the answers and also used a slightly different English expression. This was obviously an error. The US Prosecutor approached the Bench and they called me there as well.

The matter to clear up was the minute difference (maybe in shading, maybe in emphasis) between the two answers. My answer was that I felt that my translation was a closer "interpretation" of the different words used by the defendant the second time around.

The judge we were speaking to leaned forward, friendly but stern: "interpretation has the connotation of opinion and your opinion has no place in this Court". (I did not agree with him, but he was the judge!)

He instructed the Prosecutor to start this part of the questioning all over again.

Another trap that I often fell into was a psychological one, and after the trial I was told that it occurred frequently with court translators. As a matter of law, the translator must speak exactly if he or she were <u>the</u> witness. That is an "I did" translates as an "I did", NOT --"he did".

This is relatively easy to get accustomed to and to do automatically, until the witness says something that the translator finds impossible to associate with morally, finds abhorrent or offensive. Then he slips easily into "He did" instead of "I did".

This happened to me several times and the gavel always sounded to interrupt the proceedings. A judge then instructed us to which point to return in the questioning.

After one such slip, the defense attorney insisted that I be sworn in again to be reminded of my sworn duties.

The trial lasted about one week to ten days. All SS men were found guilty and got 5-10 years in prison. "My" man who was a sergeant and in command of the SS detachment, was also found responsible for never attempting to stop the excesses of the SS under his command. He was sentenced to 20 years.

I thought he deserved to die, but as they told me several times, the court was not interested in the opinion of the translator.

"DOES HE HAVE A GUN"?

Since I had been turned over to the SS in Komarom during the fall of 1944, I had had no news of my parents. I last saw them when I left our apartment in Budapest during (I believe) May of 1944.

I never had in mind to return permanently to Hungary, and since liberation I had been planning to emigrate to the US.

There was no postal service to speak of in Europe and I tried several times to get in touch with them through UNRRA (United Nations Relief and Rehabilitation Administration) and through the IRO (International Refugee Organization), but I never got a response.

I got the idea of visiting Budapest and hopefully my parents about a week after the Post Utilities Section was assigned several cars by the US motor pool.

It was evident that if I wanted to visit and come back out of Russian-occupied communist Hungary, I had to play the role of an American soldier.

The car with US markings was step number one.

It requires some explanation where these cars came from. As I described before, the concentration camp was surrounded by a large, probably divisional, SS military installation. The SS used --- and left behind --- hundreds of cars of every description, German military vehicles and some fancy civilian cars used by the SS command.

These cars were registered and refurbished as necessary by the US motor pool and by the vehicle maintenance department of the Post Utilities Section. They were then assigned to US military personnel and to people such as us who worked for the US military. Since the German military or civilian license plates had been removed from these cars, they were supplied with US Army serial numbers and after a paint job were given the US Army insignias of the white stars.

I discussed the idea of going to Hungary with Marty, a good friend, and former inmate of the concentration camp. He was working with me and headed the automotive repair services of the Post Utilities Department. I did not dare to make the trip alone and Marty was my age and had an adventurous mind. In addition he had the advantage of speaking Slovakian.

He agreed and we made the plans together. The US uniforms were no problem. The former inmates of the concentration camp working for the US Army were issued hundreds of sets of uniforms, naturally without insignia.

Passes were a more difficult issue. Most of Austria was in the Russian zone of occupation. The official border crossing-point for US troops into Vienna, which at that time was under four power occupation (similar to Berlin) was the Danube bridge at Linz. The farthest point east to which the so-called "US Gray Military Pass" could be issued was Vienna.

We were not entitled to such passes but our connections with Military Post Transportation Officer (the issuer of Trip Tickets) were good enough to obtain "Gray Passes" during a lunch period when the lieutenant was not at his desk.

We made out the passes Linz-Vienna-Budapest. Of this, Budapest was a nonsense because only Russian authorities were authorized to issue passes beyond Vienna.

Our plans were built mostly on hoping.

We hoped to avoid all road blocks.

We hoped that an official-looking paper would be accepted by most Russian soldiers regardless of what was on it.

We hoped that Marty's knowledge of a Slavic language would help.

We hoped that a few wrist watches and many packages of American cigarettes, known to be great barter items for the Russians, would help us through difficult situations.

Our main preparations were hopes!

The car filled with gas and several extra five- gallon cans of gas between the seats covered by US Army blankets, we set out early one morning.

The first Russian border guard was at the far end of the Danube bridge at Linz, as expected.

We did not count on problems at Linz because the four power occupation of Vienna was supplied via this road and the Russian soldiers were familiar with the Gray Passes.

To conserve our gas reserves, in Vienna we filled up at one of the US Military gas stations without complications.

Then we followed the highway to Budapest and ran into our first encounter with Russian border guards at the Austrian-Hungarian border, two soldiers one at each side of the road, partially behind sand bags. Marty was driving and came to a stop waving the two passes in his hand. I did not notice when he prepared for it, but his short sleeved US military shirt allowed two watches to be clearly seen on his wrist.

The Russian took the passes and walked over to the other soldier, where they had a long conference (at least it seemed long to us). They came over and both of them started to talk. I did not understand a single word, but as I saw Marty taking off the watches I felt that things were going in the right direction. He handed them the watches and said something in a Slavic language that they seemed to understand. They gave us back our passes and waved us on.

"What would you have done if they had taken the watches and not let us go?" I asked Marty.

"I would have had to bargain more carefully the next time, but hopefully there will be no next time," he answered, laughing.

In a short time we drove through Gyoer, which is the biggest town between Vienna and Budapest. As we left the eastern part of the town behind us, we thought that it would be clear sailing to Budapest.

We underestimated the Russians!!

A road block loomed ahead of us behind a slight curve, just as the main street of the town opened into the highway. We turned to each other and, without saying anything, it became clear to the both of us that this was the logical place for the road block.

Road blocks within the town would not have made sense. Any guard post could have been easily by-passed by taking a number of parallel side streets.

This road block appeared to be a sizable permanent installation with a double bar blocking the entire width of the road and with groups of Russian soldiers on both sides.

No bargaining here!

We showed our passes to the soldier who approached us and he instantly called for his superior. He was young and was probably a lieutenant. He looked at our US Gray Passes and said these fateful words in fluent English: Vienna OK, Budapest NOT OK. It was painfully evident that, whether he spoke English or not, he knew the rule that the Gray Passes were valid only as far as Vienna.

The officer called a soldier to act as an interpreter. His knowledge of English was limited but quite adequate to understand us, although at times we had to repeat our sentences in several different ways. At the same time Marty justly reasoned that we must appear as American as possible and refrained from using his Slovakian.

While the officer left to make some phone calls, the interpreter told us to pull the car to the side of the road and wait.

The officer was back and told us through the interpreter that we were under arrest and a guard would accompany us to either the Vienna or the Budapest "Kommandatura". It somehow seemed that the choice of where we would be taken was up to us.

We had originally set out to go to Budapest and with or without a Russian guard that appeared to be the logical choice, so we responded that we would be happy to explain everything at the Russian Command in Budapest.

We spent the night in the car, it was a beautiful summer night and after making sure that our spare five-gallon gas cans were tightly closed and well covered by the blankets, we tried to think out our situation.

If they accepted our response and the Russian guard accompanied us to Budapest we must somehow get in touch with the US military mission there. The eventuality of our needing the help of the US Military never came up in our original planning, and beyond the fact that there was a US Military Mission in Budapest, we did not know anything about it (including its location).

We came up with no plan and there was nothing left but to react to any eventuality as it might arise.

Our situation was precarious at best.

We had been born in Hungary so we could be justifiably considered Hungarians and could be detained as such.

Our US military uniforms were a charade.

Our Gray Passes were genuine, but officially we could not have them because we were not Americans.

Very early next morning the Russian interpreter-soldier showed up, accompanied by a young Russian (may have been a corporal). The interpreter told us that the corporal would take us to Budapest. Marty was driving, I moved to the back seat. The Russian made himself comfortable on the front passenger seat and placed his gun on his lap.

We were on our way. The early start was fortunate because this should get us into Budapest not later than early afternoon and we were still thinking of contacting the US Military Mission --- somehow.

Marty tried to talk to the Russian and had some luck with his Slovakian.

I, of course, did not understand a single word and Marty occasionally switched to English to bring me up-to-date. The fact that we spoke English with a distinct Hungarian accent was no problem, as far as the Russian was concerned all English sounded alike.

It seemed that our corporal had no idea where in Budapest the Russian Kommandatura was, where he was to take us.

We were making good headway and stopped at a small (and very primitive) restaurant along the road. This was an unexpectedly good idea of Marty's for two reasons. Firstly it appeared that even the poor soup, bread and a few green peppers were a welcome meal to the Russian. More importantly, Marty got up from the table and went into the kitchen and came back with a bottle about half full of something which he referred to as vodka. The owner was right behind him with three small brandy glasses. He poured, the Russian drank heartily and we made believe that we were joining him.

After his second or third drink, the corporal became more friendly and I distinctly remember that he was sitting with an arm around Marty's shoulders. On the principle that one should strike the iron while it is hot, I reached into my pocket and came out with a wristwatch which I put into the corporal's hand. He was happy as a child and thanked us profusely (in Russian).

It was time to go if we wanted to get to Budapest during office hours.

As we got closer to Budapest I started to become more and more concerned. We had two adversaries. Obviously the Russians, but suddenly the Hungarians loomed even more dangerously.

I could not forget Hungarian anti-Semitism in general and in my mind's eye I saw the headlines of one of the Hungarian newspapers on the day before I had been conscripted into the forced labor service of the Hungarian Army:

"You cannot make bacon from a dog
You cannot make a Hungarian of a Jew."

Our only possible way out was the US Military Mission.

Fate came to our assistance. The car's engine coughed a few times and stopped. Marty and I jumped out of the car. We knew that the problem was caused by a small amount of water in the carburetor. It happened fairly often. In the US army, gasoline was often filled into five gallon tanks which stood in the open and contained traces of water. The water ultimately ended up in a carburetor and stopped the ignition. Engines those days were much simpler than now and with a screw driver and an adjustable wrench you could clean a carburetor in ten minutes.

This gave us a few minutes to think and talk. It also gave us an idea. We knew that gasoline and tires were unbelievably precious commodities for the Russian army and we based our plan on this fact. As we reassembled the carburetor I asked Marty how much gas we had in the tank. What I really wanted to know what the fuel gauge showed. "A little less than a quarter tank". Excellent, I said, we will tell him that we are nearly out of gas and one of the tires is losing air. We can only get assistance at the US Military Mission motor pool. To make the show complete, before getting back into the car we kicked the tires and looked and talked concerned.

After he started the engine, Marty did his best to explain the situation in Slovakian to the Russian. At first the corporal objected loudly, I only understood the many "nyets", but when Marty asked him whether a US military vehicle could be filled up with gas at the Kommandatura, he confirmed that that was unlikely and agreed to allow us to go to the US Military Mission first to fill up and have the tire checked and to continue from there to the Kommandatura.

We were in the outskirts of Budapest and since I knew the City I took over the driving. But where is the US Military Mission and how would we find out. The language was surely no problem.

Then I started to notice that some pedestrians were smiling and waving at us. Clearly any US presence was a welcome sight in Budapest. This encouraged me and I slowed down near a middle aged man as he was waiting to cross the street. I asked him in Hungarian where the US Military Mission was. It was amazing to watch his face. First, I think he assumed he did not understand me because he knew that he did not understand English. Obviously I must have been speaking English because I was an American. Then his brain switched in the wrong direction and he started to put a few words together in English. I interrupted him and told him that I had been born in Budapest and what he imagined hearing as Hungarian was really just that.

He immediately gave me the address and was about to give directions. When I told him I knew how to get there, he looked somewhat disappointed. He obviously thought that we were US soldiers and was not willing to give up the opportunity to communicate Hungarian with Americans. I called his attention to the Russian solder sitting next to me and drove on.

I had no trouble finding the US Mission and our car fitted naturally among the various others with US markings on the parking lot.

All three of us went into the large foyer and I left Marty with the Russian and moved over to two or three sergeants sitting at a long counter at impressive telephone consoles. I did my best to explain our predicament to them quickly.

He said we had better see the colonel and mentioned, to my surprise, the very common Hungarian family name of Szabo.

He called the colonel and gave him a very abbreviated version of our story.

"Have the two fellows in US uniforms come up"

"Have the Russian wait in the lobby".

With some difficulty, Marty made the Russian soldier understand that we had to go upstairs to request and to sign for the gasoline and a tire and that we would be back shortly. This seemed to satisfy him and he sat down as usual with his gun in his lap.

Colonel Szabo, whose family must have been of Hungarian origin, considering his name, had his office on one of the top floors with a magnificent view of the Hungarian parliament building.

We gave him a completely true and honest description of all the facts.

We were former inmates of Dachau, and were now working for the US Army Corps of Engineers in Dachau. We decided on this obviously ill-advised trip just to meet my parents, or to find out what had happened to them if they were no longer alive. We had run into a Russian road block and were arrested and are now being accompanied by a Russian soldier who is to take us to the Russian command.

As a pleasant surprise, the colonel was most sympathetic with our cause.

"Where is the Russian" -- he asked the desk-Sergeant who accompanied us up from the foyer.

"In the lobby" was the answer.

"Did he check in his gun before entering this building?"

"No!" the Sergeant responded "he had it in his lap when I last saw him"

The colonel smiled and looked at us.

"You realize that you must leave Hungary as soon as possible".

He turned to me: " I can give you about 24 hours to look for your parents. That is just about as long as I can detain your Russian soldier for bearing a fire-arm when entering this building, which has the extraterritorial rights of an embassy.

At this moment, the sergeant knew what to do and made a phone call to the guard desk in the lobby.

The Colonel continued that he would describe a route out of Hungary where there was no known Russian presence.

"If you are lucky, you can make it to the British zone of occupation in Austria without running into any Russians and from there-on you are reasonably safe with your Gray Passes.

In staccato sentences he continued:

"The sergeant will help you fill up your tank"

"You never met me".

"I wish you good luck!"

As he stretched out his arm to shake hands he handed me a slip of paper with a few words scribbled on it. On the way down in the elevator I looked at the paper and recognized the names of some small Hungarian towns west of the Danube toward the Austrian border, much farther south than the main Vienna Budapest highway where we had come in.

We came out of the building of the US Military Mission through a back door and never saw our Russian guard again. In many ways we had learned to like him. He was not rude and he always made us understand that he was just carrying out orders. He was a simple "farm-boy" type youngster who tried to understand what was happening around him. I hope he was not punished badly for not being able to deliver his prisoners. (Although we surely would not have wanted to be delivered!!!!)

I headed the car up the Andrassy ut (renamed to something entirely different by the Hungarian Communist regime) and drove toward our apartment.

As I stopped at the traffic light before turning left toward our street, my father crossed the avenue in front of our car!!!

I did not know how to handle such an unexpected surprise meeting. I pulled the car to the curb and parked it. I do not know why, but intuitively I figured that the best approach was to get ahead of my father, turn around, and let him recognize me. This plan may not have been clever, but as it turned out the surprise was not total. My parents had seen my name about one week before on a list of survivors of Dachau, distributed by the Jewish Council of Budapest. Meeting my father on the street was not exactly fortunate, since he had a heart condition. It would have been better to drive to the apartment and wait for his return. However, at that moment I did not know that my mother had also survived the ghetto, the persecution, the hiding in attics and the moving nightly from one Christian friend to the other.

Not to mention the fear whenever the door bell rang and being on the verge of being arrested and bargaining for your freedom.

In any event, my father first did not appear to believe his eyes. Then we both stretched out our arms toward each other. We got into the car for the short drive home.

I found both my mother and father in reasonably good health.

I briefly related the story of our arrest by the Russians and said that we must be on our way out of Hungary the next day. This news was hard for them to take, but amazingly, as only loving parents are capable of doing, they said that they would rather see me in America than in Communist Hungary. Only my mother lived to see us and her grandchildren in New York.

I have no idea, how, but it turned out that several people knew about my good fortune of having a responsible position working for the US Army. These included people that I did not even know. I found out later that most of them had an ulterior motive.

It might have been better if my mother had not been so forthright, but whoever she promised to notify if she heard of me, she called immediately.

Marty and I made it clear to everybody that we were going to leave between 10 and 11 next morning. The visits of my childhood friends, real and imaginary, started within minutes.

A young and dear childhood friend, Leslie Dan, who lived in the neighborhood, showed up first. I was happy to see him because although he was a couple of years younger than I, we had grown up together and it was an emotional reunion for us.

Leslie related, if I recall correctly, that he had been in hiding in Budapest during the entire German occupation and the terror reign of the Hungarian collaborationist Nazi government. He survived by his sheer willpower and initiative with "only" emotional scars. Leslie was always a results-oriented survivor.

Another visitor, Maurice Schafer, was unknown to me personally. He was an older brother of a former Dachau inmate who worked for us in one of the automotive departments of the US Army Post Utilities Section.

His request was no less than that we should smuggle him out of Hungary. Even with all the help of false rationalizations, I still can not explain why I did what I did in those days. However, Marty and I agreed to smuggle him out of Hungary. I have thought of this hundreds of times since and never found an even remotely justifiable reason to have taken the risk. It was asking for Siberia or worse!!

After a tearful farewell from my parents, during which I saw my father the for the last time, following last minute preparations, we left next morning with Maurice in the rear seat.

Before getting out of the city we drove by a stationery store and purchased some good road maps of Western Hungary and Eastern Austria.

On an empty street Maurice moved back to the trunk of the car in case we ran into a Russian road block at the bridge crossing the Danube between Pest and Buda.

Our trip turned out to be as eventless as a trip can be under constant stress and mental pressure. We were on secondary highways which in Hungary after World War II were occasionally nothing more than partially dirt roads with "reminders" that they used to be paved. We drove slowly, not only because the type of road did not allow any speed, but also because we wanted to allow ourselves as much time for thinking and maneuvering as possible, should we spot a road block.

We fully realized that it was unlikely that we would spot a road block before our gray BMW with the white stars was noticed. We played the long-shot that if there was a check point with some cars backed up, we could turn around and move into a rural side road before we were seen.

Tracking the names of the villages on the detailed map on my lap, I realized that we were closing in on the Austrian border. Some of the village names were already posted in Hungarian and German.

We stopped and Maurice climbed back into the trunk.

We did not know what was waiting for us, so there was no way to plan. When we passed the village of Koermend, which was shown on colonel Szabo's list, we knew that we were in the border zone and there must be a check point ahead of us.

It showed up shortly at a slight elevation ahead of us. The pole was standing upright, not blocking the road. The pole was painted red, white and green, the Hungarian colors. These were not Russians!!. A few soldiers were standing around showing no interest whatsoever in us. I doubt very much that they knew what their duties were or whether they had any.

We slowed down, we waved, they waved and I slowly accelerated.

We were aware that we were driving through a politically unstable and troubled area. The south east part of Austria was the British zone of occupation, but Hungary was in the Russian sphere of influence and we were still concerned about Russians patrolling the border area.

We were waved through the Austrian border station and after a few miles we thought that it was safe enough for Maurice to again climb out of the trunk.

Maurice climbed into and out-of the trunk, it seems, an endless number of times. This description of our journey and my memory do not account for all occasions this had happened.

From some British flags and occasional British military vehicles on the streets it was clear that we were at least temporarily safe.

As soon as we entered the city of Graz, with ample indications of British military presence, we felt safe enough and decided to take an over-night rest in a small local inn. Our safest course of action appeared to be to head north and get onto the west-bound Vienna-Linz-Salzburg "Autobahn", as if coming from Vienna. On the highway, Marty and I were reasonably safe with our Gray Passes and the "only" problems remaining were unexpected Russian check points and the discovery of Maurice. The main obstacle to get over was the Russian zone crossing point on the Danube bridge near the city of Linz. There was no other way to get him across that check point but to hide him in the trunk of the car. His discovery would automatically implicate us as smugglers.

As we got closer to Linz, I started to grasp the unbelievable stupidity of taking the risk of smuggling someone through the Russian check-point in the trunk of the car.

We were moving at about 50 miles an hour toward the point of no return at Linz, with Maurice in the trunk.

There were a few vehicles before us at the check point and we shut off our engine and waited. Two Russians climbed up on the platform of an American army truck, walked around and jumped off.

The car in front of us had Austrian plates and the Russians made the driver get out of the car. They bent down, looked in, looked under the car, gave the man back his papers and let him through.

It was our turn. I moved up slowly, smiled broadly and handed out our US Gray Military Passes. The Russian appeared to examine the passes carefully, walked over to the other soldier, came back behind our car, banged his hand on the trunk, gave me back the passes and waved us on.

These few minutes of extreme stress, which I will never ever forget, would have been enough for a heart attack for anybody in or past middle age.

On the US side of the bridge they stamped our passes "Returned" and we were on our way back on the Salzburg-Munich Autobahn and its various bypasses toward Dachau.

According to military procedure, I turned in our Gray Passes to the Transportation Office next day.

Naturally, the only event which I discussed was the stated purpose of the trip, meeting my parents.

As the T. O. looked at the passes and saw that the return crossing point was the US Station at Linz, he asked what appeared to be a weird question.

"Did the Russian bang on your trunk?"

I looked puzzled and almost said no, but I remembered that he had indeed done so!

"Yes he did", I finally responded.

"They usually do" the Transportation Officer answered, "because an empty trunk sounds different, from a full one".

Only then did I realize how close Linz was to Siberia!!!

If Maurice said an informal thank you I do not remember.

I got him a job in the Post Utilities Section and he spent several years there until he emigrated to South America, where later he did very well financially. I met him once or twice in New York.

I do not know whether I am owed a "thank you" for giving him a chance at a new life or for risking my life doing it, but if I do, I never got it!

MORE VISITORS

My short and abruptly ended visit to Hungary resulted in more exaggerated stories about my position with the US Army than if I had stayed in Budapest for a while and had a chance to explain it all.

Distant relatives, friends, friends of friends, showed up from Hungary having decided that due to my "influential position" (which was nothing more than a good job), Dachau was the most logical staging area for their emigration to the free world.

Indeed, the Munich-Dachau area was an important center of operations for several refugee organizations. The United Jewish Appeal, The National Catholic Welfare Conference and many others operated within the framework of UNRRA and the IRO, to organize, assemble and start refugee transports to the United States, Canada, Australia, South America, etc.

My young childhood friend from Budapest, Leslie Dan, became one of my long time guests in Dachau.

The first step in any emigration registration process was to qualify as a Displaced Person (in other words a refugee). The simplest and most natural way to be a Displaced Person (DP) was to have been in a concentration camp. Since most camp records were incomplete and since several duplicates existed which usually did not agree with each other, it was not difficult to "assist" someone in appearing on a list of camp inmates and to obtain a certificate to that effect (and thus help them qualify as a Displaced Person).

The US Army Post Utilities Section in Dachau administered and even constructed much of the living quarters for its employees and I had no trouble arranging for decent quarters for my various "visitors" from Hungary.

The US Army provided excellent food and cafeteria facilities. I made available mess-hall passes for all my guests.

Another important service of the US Army Post Utilities section was a tailor and shoe-repair shop. This was originally intended only to do minor alterations, repairs and ironing for US Army personnel, but grew into a fully fledged tailor and cobbler shop, occasionally doing fancy, exclusive work for US officers. Naturally, since the shop was within the framework of the Post Utilities Section, my visitors were also supplied with it's products of suits and shoes.

I took personal satisfaction in being in a position to assist all who came to me.

For most of my guests I also arranged for jobs with the US Army, which always allowed them enough free time to pursue their emigration goals.

Directly or indirectly, if needed, I assisted my visitors in legitimizing their status as displaced persons and thus to become eligible for their emigration objectives.

Not all of them found success in the New World, but all of them found freedom.

I am happy that my friend, Leslie L Dan *, who asked my support in Dachau and in whose emigration I was of meaningful help, became a human and financial success in the New World and one of the great Jewish philanthropists. I am glad that I played my modest role in enabling him to bring to fruition his natural talent and ambitions.

Helping him turned out to be one of the most important things that I did.

* Leslie L. Dan is Chairman and CEO of NOVOPHARM, one of the largest manufacturers of generic drugs in the pharmaceutical industry. The company's headquarters is in Toronto, Canada, with several factories in many parts of the world.

POSTSCRIPT

On the previous pages I touched upon the fact that frequently I came perilously close to dying during the period of the holocaust.

The Hungarians held a gun to my head on many occasions. In Dachau I survived typhus and typhoid fever, which killed about 80-90% of those who were infected.

I was on the verge of being turned over to the SS guards in Dachau several times.

I could have been discovered hiding with Stan in the "Leichenwagen" (corpse truck) and shot on the spot.

I volunteered to take part in an "information gathering" action for the Allies which clearly put my life in jeopardy.

I risked discovery and possibly death when I worked out an elaborate plan to find out the secret of the "**NAZI GOLD**".

I helped with an escape from Dachau for which there was only one penalty, ---death.

Smuggling a person out of Communist Hungary through Russian check-points called for ----at least----a long stay in Siberia.

I do not think that I was either clever or lucky to have survived.

**SOMEBODY UP THERE LIKED ME
(AND I HOPE STILL DOES).
I AM THANKFUL THAT I COULD MAKE SOME
POSITIVE CONTRIBUTIONS TO THE CAUSE OF
HUMANITY AND WAS GIVEN THE
OPPORTUNITY TO CHRONICLE MY
EXPERIENCES DURING THE HOLOCAUST, FIFTY
YEARS AFTER THEY OCCURRED.**

Appendix

Reference to Footnote #1

Chapter: Information Gathering (Spying?)

These notes are based on the author's analysis of the transcripts of the Nuremberg trials as reproduced in the National Archives.

The introduction to the publication is Copyright by John Mendelsohn, New York: Garland 1982

Oswald Pohl (Lieutenant General/ *Obergruppenfuehrer)* was chief of the SS Economic and Administrative Main Office. (WVHA). The relatively harmless sounding name indicating some type of beaurocratic/administrative function was hiding the fact that **this office was in charge of all concentration camps.**

It was one of the eleven main offices (HA-s) reporting directly to Himmler.

Pohl was a devoted Nazi and his career with the SS was that of a fast rising star. Between 1934 and 1940 he rose from colonel to a top general of the SS.

His title and position was;

Supreme Administrative Officer of the SS.

He was tried in Nuremberg by a US Military Court. His defense was based on the argument that it was Himmler and Himmler alone who ordered the liquidation of the Jews. He claimed ignorance or essentially no involvement in the 'final solution'. However, he seemed to be able to estimate that about three million Jews were liquidated in Auschwitz.

He also admitted that he was in Auschwitz during the summer months of 1944 and knew **'exactly'** (this is the officially translated word from the transcript of his trial) about the liquidation of the Hungarian Jews there. He admitted having personally witnessed trains arriving from Hungary and Jews being taken to Krematoriums.

Pohl acknowledged that he knew jewelry and gold teeth that were taken from people in the concentration camps had been transferred to the German central Bank *(Reichsbank)* .

The following are the summarized findings (freely paraphrased) by the US Military Tribunal in Nuremberg.

"Under the command of Pohl a ruthless plan was developed of extracting from concentration camp inmates their last ounce of energy in furtherance of the *Reich's* war plans.

Armed with this power Pohl energetically set about driving the inmates to the limit of endurance in order to further the economic and war efforts of the *Reich*.

As of July of 1944 there were 20 concentration camps and 165 labor camps supervised by Pohl's Main Office. In some instances he recommended appointments and transfers of camp commanders who were the slave drivers in the camps.

On several occasions Pohl's interest lead him to inspect concentration camps in person. He visited Auschwitz, Ravensbruck, Dachau and Oranienburg.

Pohl ordered that the working hours in concentration camps be 11 hours six days a week and half a day on Sunday.

There was doubtless no other person in Germany who knew as much about all the details of the concentration camps as Pohl.

Leaving all other considerations aside, Pohl stands before this Tribunal as an admitted slave driver on a scale never before known."

Note by the author:: "I personally visited Pohl's lavishly appointed chalet located in a small forest within the SS camp in Dachau, a few days after the war's end (it was less than a mile from the former concentration camp). It surely created a 'lived-in' appearance. I have seen a wide selection of uniforms, boots and other personal items. Pictures of political and personal subjects covered all available wall-space. The house was dominated by a large reception area with a huge impressive ornamental wood desk at one end. Two autographed and dedicated pictures of Hitler and Himmler in glass stands were located at two corners of the desk. A richly equipped kitchen and pantry, with gold rimmed and monogrammed dishes and goblets, (all featuring the swastika) rounded out, the interior of a house, which looked much more than a lodging for short temporary periods.

I believe that *Obergruppenfuehrer* Pohl spent more than 'occasional' periods in Dachau (as he stated at his war crimes trial)".

In an affidavit to the Court dated June 1946 Pohl stated that he was aware of the medical experiments performed in Dachau (sterilization, high altitude, freezing, malaria, typhus, sea water, Polygal, etc.) He accompanied Himmler to observe high altitude experiments on prisoners in Dachau.

Pohl was found guilty by the Nuremberg US Military Tribunal and was condemned to death. He was hanged in Landsberg on June 7, 1951.

> **Reference to Footnote #2**

Chapter: The "Nazi Gold"

> All quotations COPYRIGHT ©
> **THE NEW YORK TIMES COMPANY.**

In the quotations which follow some bold face type was added by the author to emphasize subjects which have a direct relation to the contents of this book.

> **THE NEW YORK TIMES**
> May 8, 1997
> David E Sanger

WASHINGTON-- In a searing historical indictment, a US government report concluded on Wednesday that the Swiss government deliberately failed to respect a 1946 agreement to return **hundreds of millions of dollars in assets that Nazi Germany looted from European banks and Holocaust victims** and the United States stood by.

The newest revelation contained in the report was that a small but significant percentage of the "monetary **gold**" Switzerland accepted from the Nazis included jewelry and **gold teeth-fillings** stolen from **Holocaust victims, some of it apparently removed from their remains at Nazi concentration camps.**

It has long been known that the Nazis took **gold fillings from the teeth of Holocaust victims,** along with **wedding rings, and other jewelry they confiscated**. But the report for the first time establishes that this **gold** was mingled with the "monetary **gold**" deposited in Swiss banks. The Swiss government on Wednesday called this "grave news of the most shocking nature."

Excerpts from a State Department report published on Wednesday (May 7, 1997) about the disposition of assets looted by Nazi Germany during World War II.

These goods were stolen from governments and civilians in the countries Germany overran and from Jewish and non-Jewish victims of the Nazis alike, **including Jews murdered in extermination camps, from whom everything was taken, down to the gold fillings of their teeth.**

The report concluded that there is no evidence that the Swiss banks knew of the gruesome origins of this **gold**.

THE NEW YORK TIMES   October 7, 1997   David E Sanger

WASHINGTON-- A study conducted for the World Jewish Congress concludes that **Nazi Germany looted at least $8.5 billion in gold between 1933 and 1945 and for the first time estimates the amount --- nearly a third --- that came from individuals and private businesses rather than central banks.**

A study released by the Clinton administration earlier this year came up with similar estimates of the amount of looted gold Nazi Germany seized during the war, and later sent to Switzerland and other nations for safekeeping or to pay for war materiel. It also concluded that so-called "monetary gold," --- gold stolen from central banks --- had been intermingled with "non-monetary gold," or **gold taken from individuals, and, in some cases tooth fillings of Holocaust victims.**

THE NEW YORK TIMES   November 2, 1997   David E Sanger

WASHINGTON --A report issued by the Clinton administration this year concludes that the German mint often took the **gold** that the German troops stole from the central banks of Europe and melted it together with **gold of more gruesome variety: the tooth-fillings, wedding rings and other jewelry of death- camp victims.**

THE NEW YORK TIMES   December 2, 1997   Alan Cowell

LONDON-- Swiss historians said Monday that the amount of **gold** stolen from concentration camp prisoners and other victims of **Nazi** Germany was much higher than previously assumed by other experts -- totaling some $146 million at 1945 prices.

The report said a much larger proportion of **gold** that went through **Nazi** coffers during World War II -- around one sixth -- was so-called **victim gold,** as opposed to **gold** looted from central banks or acquired from Germany's own reserves.

Secretary of State Madeleine K Albright
Excerpts from Remarks Before Members of the Swiss Parliament Bern, Switzerland, November 15, 1997
As released by the Office of the Spokesman US Department of State

---

.....the Swiss National Bank accepted large amounts of looted gold from Nazi Germany that, together with trade and vital commodities from other neutral nations, helped sustain the German war effort; and the Swiss National Bank resisted efforts after the war for full restitution of the stolen assets as private Swiss banks failed to provide full openness with respect to dormant accounts......

Reference to Footnote #3

Chapter: War Crimes Trials

ILSE KOCH, "THE BITCH OF BUCHENWALD", was accused to have ordered the manufacture of lampshades, covers for photo albums, gloves, etc., from the tanned human skins of deceased prisoners.

She was convicted by the US tribunal in Dachau to life in prison.

The sentence was commuted by General LUCIUS D CLAY the US Commander in Europe to a short prison term!!!

Frau KOCH was later sentenced to life imprisonment by a German court.

She committed suicide about 20 years later in 1967.

About the Author

Steven Wassermann was born at Budapest, Hungary in 1924. His father was a well to do textile merchant, but his financial fortunes deteriorated as anti-Semitism got stronger in Hungary.

The family was not particularly religious and like most Jews in Hungary, Steve, during his childhood, believed that his nationality was Hungarian and his religion Jewish.

Due to the proximity and influence of Nazi Germany, the Hungarian government (with few notable exceptions) became increasingly anti-Semitic and the idea of duality of nationality and religion was no longer accepted. A Jew was a Jew -- and not a Hungarian.

The Germans occupied Hungary in March of 1944 and together with tens of thousands of Jewish males he was conscripted into a "forced labor service" operating under the command of the Hungarian army.

70 percent of the Hungarian Jews, 569,000 souls, perished in the Holocaust.

Upon immigrating to the US he worked during the day and obtained his engineering degrees by studying at night.

During a distinguished professional career with the MERGENTHALER LINOTYPE Company, Mr. Wassermann served as Vice President of Group Operations of the Mergenthaler Division of the ALLIED SIGNAL Corporation He is the author of several books and articles on technical and management subjects.

Mr. Wassermann and his wife, Valerie, live in New York. They have two grown children.